Tales of Erana: Just One Mistake

A. L. Butcher

A Tales of Erana Novella

Copyright © A. L. Butcher 2014, 2017, 2021, 22, 23, 24
ISBN 13: 978-1546421726
ISBN-10 1546421726

Title: Tales of Erana: Just One Mistake

Author: A. L. Butcher

All rights reserved.

The right of A. L. Butcher to be identified as the author of this work has been asserted in accordance with Section 77 of the Copyright, Designs and Patents Act 1988.

The world of Erana and the characters herein are the property of the author. Any similarity to actual persons is purely coincidental.

Base cover art © Vallentin Vassileff – adobe.com and adapted by S. Frost and A.L. Butcher.

Originally published in short form in Nine Heroes: Tales of Heroic Fantasy published by Stencil Press 2014.

Revised and expanded 2017 for this format.

Part One

It was proving to be a reasonably successful night for the bard, at least if success was measured by earning enough coin to pay for his paltry accommodation and not being robbed or stabbed. A victory was still a victory, no matter how small, Coel knew. Every day was both a blessing and a curse depending on one's point of view. Coel had soon discovered those who did not learn fast had few days left to them, and survival was a deadly game with lousy odds. So far, he was winning, but only just. Life had been a severe teacher of late and lessons could be terminal. Bitterly, he thought the gods had a twisted sense of humour, and he hoped they were enjoying the spectacle.

The catcalls from his audience had been replaced by the rowdiness of inebriated men listening to songs of love and the conquest of wenches. He'd played to worse. More than once he'd had to grab his rebec and run for it on previous nights, and in previous venues. Coel had started this evening with songs known by all and now the sound of thirty or forty voices rose, if not in unison, then at least in merry and very loud enthusiasm. Some of the lyrics were of the more vulgar variety but Coel simply nodded and continued to play and sing, after all, he was a servant to the music, nothing more, and well he knew it. Magic, for such it was, went where it pleased and showed itself where it could in a land where magic was illegal. Many held talents beyond the norm and those who were lucky, or clever soon learned to disguise them. Those who were not lucky or clever rarely lived long enough to rue.

The tavern girl, Elsa, who was adept at fending off wandering hands and immune to the lewd jokes, winked at him and brought a large dish of steaming meat stew. He was favoured – this was identifiable meat and not that saved for the less popular patrons and workers, labelled simply as 'meat'. Once he'd made the mistake of asking its source. That night he'd been hungry through choice, but now Coel knew the desperate would eat almost anything to survive. In such a place, and such a life, choices were few. He'd even eaten rat and rotting vegetables when times were lean and coin sparse. Once he'd supped on fine meats, expensive wines, and the most exotic of fruits. That life was far away, and in the darkness and fear of his current existence, Coel wondered if it had ever really existed.

Painted women of negotiable affection mingled among the drinkers, hoping for their own variety of business. There would be a few warm beds that night. Coel grinned, these women were old hands in this place of ale and amusement and light-fingered with it. A few newcomers would find more than just their needs satisfied. Such patrons as these did not bother to report a theft here and there. It was an occupational hazard, and besides, they had their own secrets and their own burdens. Many simply returned the favour when the opportunity presented itself.

Coel's life now was surprisingly risky, after all, it was not as though he could just ask the Order of Witch-Hunters for support when he was robbed. The Witch-Hunters tended to ask more awkward questions than Coel was prepared to answer and the brutality of their 'hospitality' was well-known. Such was life in the city, among the shadows, the outlaws and the forgotten. Coel was grateful for the latter; once, a lifetime ago he would have been outraged at such an existence. Now Coel was thankful to live another day. People in this part of Varlek asked few questions and expected fewer answers. Lies and almost-truth were stock communication here. The great city of Varlek was a jaded old crone, not the beautiful courtesan she first appeared. But she looked after her own - the low and the lost, nestled in an ancient bosom. And for that too Coel thanked the gods.

Law in Erana was an iron fist clutching shackles and providing absolutely no mercy. Justice, he had heard spoken, could be bought and sold for those with the right contacts and enough coin. For most, the law was brought by the sword, and fed with fear and hatred. Innocence was a relative term.

Sometimes Coel did not even get paid, he had been chased away on more than one occasion and travelling the roads of Erana had its own level of excitement from the thieves and bandits who made a living beyond the law. It had not been long ago when he would have found such men distasteful vagabonds and rogues who deserved a noose. One mistake had changed that. Now, he was among their number. Still, he woke in the small hours of the morning seeing the blood on his hands, and the corpse at his feet. It had been an accident, so he told himself, but the blade in the fellow's guts had been Coel's and accidents were hard to prove. Many an innocent man had visited Gallows Hill with a one-way ticket, and he'd seen the elven servant blamed, and swinging at the end of a rope.

"It's just an elf, let it hang." Those were the words his father had said when Coel begged for his help. "You'll destroy us all – your mother will die of shame and your sister? Remember she weds the Lord of Anway's youngest next month. You think that will happen when news reaches him that her brother is a murderer. That elf saw you. Make it pay, it's just an elf. Elves have no rights, you know that. My word against his. There will be no contest." Coel's father was a powerful man, a respected man and one who brooked no argument. "Of course, should you rather take its place…."

Fear had twisted Coel's guts, then shame as they watched the elven man crying his innocence as the rope was put around his neck. Coel's father there watching – making sure 'justice' was done. Hidden in shadow Coel had thrown up, trembling and wretched. His mistake paid for by another. Coel had fled that night, unable to face his father, unable to face himself. One mistake, one terrible mistake. In the dark of night, and in the cold of his soul the bard asked himself was the mistake the first death or the second, or both? He'd run, from his crime and his shame.

He'd heard the widow now had a blond-haired son, but Coel dared not ask if the boy was his, he dared not return.

Coel had resorted to thievery, in fact, he had soon found he was willing to do almost anything to eat and to live another day, although he knew his life was forfeit. He was now reasonably adept at being light-fingered, or perhaps he was just lucky. He was, after all, still alive. Drunks were the easiest target, and he rarely took more than a few coins, or small trinkets unlikely to be missed immediately. Heart pounding, the first time he had been forced to steal Coel had been sure the whole world heard as he slipped a trembling hand into the loose pockets of a rich merchant as he bustled past in the market. That theft had netted him enough coin to eat for almost a week and a new string and soft leather bag for his rebec. Given a choice, the profession which would not leave him at the end of a noose was preferable – his music. There was not always a choice. Coel now understood what it was to be hungry, cold and hunted. Life in Varlek was an unfeeling teacher.

The bard had many advantages; he was handsome with blond hair which flowed down his back and eyes of jade green, although sometimes he wished he was plainer, less conspicuous. Once he'd seen his likeness on a 'wanted notice' affixed to a post in a town near his home. Perhaps there had been another witness. He'd not stayed to discover if it was really his face or another's – maybe he'd imagined it. He did not blend in, although he'd learned to use the make-up to darken his skin and hair. A beard now covered his chin and he'd even tried the thin glass eye-lenses some used. That particular experience had left him barely able to see to play and with a headache, he couldn't tolerate. Coel was a fast learner. At least in the crowded city, there were so many bodies a man could all but disappear. One man looked much like another, at least he hoped so. Thus far he still breathed.

Once Coel had been rich, with servants who washed his clothes, fed him and warmed his bed. Once he'd been a different man; reality had been a harsh lesson. Now he was, occasionally, the bed-warmer to rich and lonely patrons, stealing trinkets and playing for drunks on a rebec which had seen better days. One mistake, one lousy mistake and his life had changed beyond recognition.

***

The attic room he rented was cold and damp but, it had to be said, the Witch-Hunters usually ignored the Stuck Pig tavern; this alone was worth the dripping roof which arched above him and whatever it was which nibbled at him from the thin mattress. The barkeep had not enquired about his background or asked to see his papers and Coel had told him no more than a form of truth; he was a bard looking for work. The clientele was not overly discerning and, when he was not playing his music or singing, no one paid him much attention, being too busy at cards or dice or with the whores. Then there were those who sought salvation or oblivion at the bottom of a barrel or the bowl of the drug-filled pipes. Heaven and hell could both be bought for a few coins. Whether one awoke after was a different matter entirely. One night the barkeep had asked Coel for help with a large, rather heavy sack. It had ended in the river, but Coel knew the weight of a man's body when he felt it. At least this poor soul could not be laid at the bard's door. Nothing more had been said about that night, but the barkeep had since become more generous with his victuals and his ale.

There were even elves and half-elves mixing with the humans, who paid no more notice to them than to any other patrons. As a human he had never considered it in his old life, it was simply how things were. Elves had brought the Plague; elves were not to be trusted. Elves were servants or slaves; property – they could be replaced. Elves had no rights, no recourse in law, as he well knew, but Coel was learning that truth had many sides. No one here asked him questions and so he held his silence in return, simply singing his songs and hoping for an opportunity to supplement his income among these elves, gamblers, whores and low-lives.

That rich man was in attendance again, Coel noted as his finished his song. This was the third or fourth night in a row he'd been here. The fellow looked a little out of place, with his fine cloak, and well-made boots and, of course, his free use of coin. Yet at the same time, his air was comfortable and easy as though he owned the place. Coel had been watching him these last few evenings; silver coins flashed from his fingers and the glint of something more, a ring of black stone and emeralds showed as the man's hand dealt and played, drank and dined in this den of sin. How long would it be before someone relieved this man of the burden of his purse or that pretty cat-shaped ring which he seemed to slip on and off a finger, almost absentmindedly? A slate grey cloak, with a cowl of black fur, hid the man's face and Coel wondered, briefly, whether he too was on the run or perhaps simply enjoyed the risk. It was a pity Coel did not consider it more carefully. In such a place as this wealth was dangerous, but ignorance more so.

Coel found it difficult to keep his eye on the stranger and pretend nothing was amiss as he played. In a place such as this who could say when a trinket disappeared? Perhaps dropped onto the floor or swept up with the coins by fellow gamblers. This ring had caught his attention, a trinket like that and he could find better lodgings, better work and better food. Perhaps he could even pay enough in the right direction to return home. Justice was a commodity as much as ale or slaves, to he who could afford it. That ring had enthralled him, though he did not know it.

Beneath the hood, the stranger's eyes watched the bard, watched him judging the target and his chances. The owner of the eyes grinned. Whatever chance the bard thought he had it would not be enough – but the game must end soon, one way or another. There was easier prey the cloaked man knew, but not quite as satisfying, or talented. So, he flashed the trinket, knowing its worth and its power and reeled in his fish whilst trying not to laugh.

Had Coel been more cautious he might have seen the fluid movements as the man dealt cards, the stalk like a cat when he walked, the belt containing small phials of black-tinted glass and the glint of metal beneath the cloak; this man was armed. This man killed others for his living. One mistake –followed by another. That was Coel's curse.

The rich man rose, swept up the coins, his own ring plus another won from someone who should have known with whom they played and unsteadily made his way out back, towards the privy. Moving to make his way upstairs back to his room, Coel stashed the rebec swiftly behind a sack and slipped out into the darkness via the small door from the kitchen. At least being resident here he had learned the layout well enough. Shadowplay had been a surprise skill, not acquired more *discovered* in that dark night which haunted his dreams; yet it had saved his life. Darkness had cloaked him, fear had made his feet fast and he had run pulling the shadows about him without realising that was what he was doing. He had no name for it, just gave thanks to whichever god was listening. Some questions were best not asked particularly in a world where such skills could bring death as well as life.

Coel was not yet, however, master of it and hoped the ale and the darkness of the night would serve him well. It was worth the risk to acquire such a trinket and find a better place than this, or to see his home again. To see her. If needs be he could simply jostle the man and be on his way. His cheap boots creaked and the few coins in his purse jingled before he shoved them deeper into the soft pocket and cursed under his breath, fortunately, the city of Varlek was noisy even at this hour.

***

Stopping to relieve himself the man leant against the wooden wall of the privy and waited. Darius, the Thiefmaster, grinned again; he had made sure the bard had seen the ring, fallen beneath its spell, although it had taken longer than he had expected for the young fellow to take the bait. Was that caution or something else, the old thief wondered? His contacts had been quite forthcoming with information about this would-be thief and the talents he might hold. Now the trap was set. The privy was cramped - just a rough shed over a pit with a bench to park one's arse upon, and three holes which dropped whatever was offered into the river. It was a good way of disposing of evidence as well as waste both the bard and the master of thieves knew.

Of course, the Thiefmaster thought, at least there *was* a privy and not the usual alleyway which sufficed for many of the taverns which were even lower on the social scale. Anyone who was too drunk or too lazy to stagger outside was welcome to use the buckets which would be collected by the tanners, alchemists and other industries which made good use of the leavings of man and beast alike. Another man staggered off, nodding drunkenly and Darius loitered, biding his time and watching the would-be thief who thought he was being stealthy. The Thiefmaster had seen worse, he'd killed better.

The touch was light, as Coel's hand slipped into Darius' pocket, at least the one which wasn't concealed. The young bard jostled close, muttering his apologies in the dark as the two men touched. Someone less experienced, or far drunker might not have noticed, not a bad attempt. Darius coughed, hacking, trying to cover the chuckle which was striving to be heard. It was not a bad place, this tavern, and it served his purpose well enough. Darius made sure it was so. Many of his employees had started their careers here, or at least the careers they now held. Even the serving wench was in his circle. She had keen ears and a good memory. Tongues wagged when ale flowed.

Coel felt the soft wool of the pocket and his long, talented fingers felt around until he found coins, and a ring, cold against his skin. He knew to hesitate would mean discovery, so he deftly rolled them along his palm and shifted position. The drunken rich man half turned and so taking the opportunity to empty his bladder Coel nodded to him as one man to another and returned to the tavern.

The House of Thieves had a number of such business establishments, unknown to the Order of Witch-Hunters, of course. Officially this was just a low tavern, in a poor and rough area of town. Sometimes the Order came to this area in pursuit of someone, more rarely they left alive and with all their limbs. Decades in the shadows had taught Darius that being ignored was to his advantage. The Order saw what it pleased them to see and Darius and his thieves knew it and used it. The fate of low-class prostitutes and cut-purses in this house of vice were far lower on the scale of importance than menacing mages and hunting elves without papers. People on the edge of the Enclave and the edge of survival rarely lived long enough to be a problem. Or so the Order believed. Reality was not always what it seemed in the land of Erana.

***

The candle spluttered in the attic as the wind curled about the badly thatched roof. Glowglobes were currently beyond Coel's means so in the small flickering circle of meagre light Coel assessed his night's takings. The tavern wench had gone to her own bed or someone else's and in many ways he was glad; any undue attention would be unwelcome in the circumstances. Coel had got away with the theft, at least he could hear no hue and cry from below or boots on the stairs. With luck, the fellow would either not miss the trinket or simply not recall his movements that evening. There had been no mistake, not this time.

Darkness oozed lazily in the remainder of the room, nosing into corners, under furniture and behind Coel, unseen, part of it detached. "That was quite a performance, bard. You have some talent, and not just your music. Although your judgement is flawed, it is never wise to steal from a thief," the voice was smooth, like liquid velvet and very sure of itself.

Coel's hand moved towards the dagger nestling in his belt; it would not be the first time he had been called on to defend himself, although that was how he had ended up in this mess he thought bitterly. Just one mistake, then another and now, it would seem, another.

"I do not know of what you speak! I am not a thief." His brain caught up and he continued, "How did you get into my room? The door was locked. I'm not a bloody fool." Coel could hear his own heart pounding. There was something about this man which frightened him. He felt like a mouse beneath the gaze of a cat. Perhaps the hangman's noose would have been the better option.

The slate-grey cloak swirled around boots of ebony leather and the cowled figure chuckled. "That lock was barely a moment's work. I must have a word with the owner of this place about his security. I have yet to find a door in Erana which will not yield to me. You may as well remove your hand from that blade, or would you bet your life you are swifter than the Thiefmaster? I doubt it, boy, I doubt it. Believe me when I say you would be dead before that knife left its scabbard. It would be a pity to waste such talent, would it not?"

Coel removed his hand from the dagger, his sense telling him that continuing to draw it would be a terminal decision. Instead, he placed his hand on the table and the voice breathed into his ear, Coel shivered, he had not heard the man move.

"I thought not. Sensible lad, if a lying one. This too can be a skill which can save your life, if it is used correctly and with assurance," Darius told him.

This menacing shape was right behind him and Coel began to turn, opening his mouth to protest, and found a gloved hand on his jaw, firm but not unduly painful. "Curious are we not? This may sometimes serve you well. As for other occasions, it is wise to accept things as they are, this is one such occasion... Coel."

The bard caught his breath, how did this man know his name? The sweat began to pool in his back, making his shirt stick unpleasantly to his skin. Had this man been hired to kill him? Had his mistake finally caught him up? Yet as Coel's brain frantically grasped at any hope and his fingers tried to overrule his brain and reach for the dagger he realised the man had said he was a thief. A robbery, that was not so bad. It would not be the first time.

"This is not merely a social call; you are honoured for the Master of Thieves does not always test a potential recruit's skills for himself."

"I usually charge for my skills, music and other kinds, if that is what you prefer. I can be flexible, and my tastes are...varied. Perhaps just this once I might offer them for free. Take the coin and the trinkets, take it all." Coel's brain finally caught up with the conversation, "What do you mean potential recruit?"

"Is that so? Well, a degree of...flexibility is often most useful. You are handsome, and personable enough, but my tastes do not run that way, at least not today and not with you. It is a simple business venture, which carries some risk, of course. A test, if you will, of how good you are. You better hope that you *are* good…" The Thiefmaster chuckled, and a chill ran down Coel's neck as the laugh held little in the way of mirth, at least not for him.

"Which, I suppose, is why you do not do it yourself? What if I refuse? I could say the ring is mine. I could say you broke into my room to steal it and murder me." Coel was not convinced but his nervous mouth was filling in the uneasy silence.

Laughing the Thiefmaster replied, "So you do have a bold streak and not just one of desperation! I had wondered if my sources were mistaken. Why should I risk my own freedom when I have others at my bidding? Besides, I have something more important requiring my attention. Should you prefer to tell your story to the Order of Witch-Hunters and sample their…hospitality I could inform them of the theft of that valuable obsidian ring. The one beneath your hand, shaped like a cat and black as night. There is not another quite like it in all the land. A friend gave it to me, a powerful friend, and should it be needed he will vouch for its true owner. I can be many men, not just the master of thieves. I am a far better liar than you, lad. I have had a good deal of practice."

The Thiefmaster was no more likely to pay a visit to the Witch-Hunters than this young thief at his mercy. If the bold young bard would hang for his crimes then Darius would do so a thousand-fold, assuming he was ever caught. Thus, he made sure he was not. Survival was a highly rated skill among the thieves and shadows at his calling, and those who did not learn it well soon ceased to be in his employ one way or another. Darius himself had survived by means of a sharp wit, a sharper blade and knowing whom to trust.

Coel sighed, knowing when he was beaten. He would be unlikely to survive a fight with this man, and another corpse at his feet, in his room, would cause far more explanation than he had the wit to endure. "So, I work for you? What, exactly, do you require of me?"

"Good lad, I knew you would see things my way. There is an item, easily pocketed, in the house of a man who needs to be inconvenienced. It is a bottle of jade crystal with a silver stopper, small but exquisite. Bring it to me, either here or at the Oaken Barrel. How you go about acquiring it I leave up to you."

"Who is this man and why do you want this item?" Coel asked, not expecting an answer.

"A… merchant, the name of Renwick. As for why? That is my business, let me just say his trade…displeases me. He is a man of means, for his business pays well. He may have a use for an entertainer in the near future."

Reaching over Darius plucked up the small obsidian ring and slipped it back onto his finger. "If you succeed your debt to me is wiped clean, I will overlook the matter of your theft and perhaps, if you please me enough, I may find more profitable work for you. I have many contacts and many powerful, if dangerous, friends. Keep that in mind, young minstrel."

Coel considered his options, "And if I fail?"

Darius grinned nastily beneath the cowl of his cloak and the darkness of the room played around his feet, caressing him like a lover. The candle flickered, almost but not quite guttering out. "Then it will no longer be a problem for either of us."

With a swirl of his cloak, the Thiefmaster turned in the doorway. "One last thing, if you decide that risking the so-called law of the Order is a preferable course of action and bring them here, or to the Oaken Barrel, know this - the shadows watch from every corner, every rooftop and every alley. We are everywhere and nowhere. Bring me the ring, bard, and perhaps your mistake will be...rectified."

Coel's cheeks flushed red, which mistake? His theft tonight or the other, darker one which plagued his dreams and made him a hunted man?

"How do I know you will not betray me?" he asked, just as the man stepped through the doorway and before Coel's brain over-ruled his mouth.

"Because I am a man of my word." With that, the fellow was gone and only darkness remained.

Part Two

Once the shock of his encounter with the man who called himself the Thiefmaster had worn off Coel had been angry, mainly at himself for being so foolish. The last few days and nights had been quite an education, Coel had previously thought the Order of Witch-Hunters ran the land and the city of Varlek, now he was not so sure. They certainly thought it was the case but as the mysterious man had informed him the shadows watched. And they did.

The ability to manipulate the darkness and the shadows was a form of magic and magic was illegal; that did not stop its use, either from those who did not care it was illegal or those desperate enough to risk it. Those who knew its secrets guarded them carefully and could spot its use among others. Coel had never dared ask how he had managed to pull the shadows about him that fateful night. Being caught using such a skill was enough to earn him a meeting with the hangman, even if nothing else he'd done would.

He suspected some of the 'shadows' which revealed themselves were for his benefit and he wondered if the Thiefmaster thought this a form of amusement. It was certainly a show of power. Coel had thought to run but once when he had found himself at the city gate he saw a figure on the roof of a nearby tower; the man had simply watched, cross-bow lazily next to him.

Then, on seeing a patrol, the man vanished and Coel asked himself if he had been there at all. Was he seeing cloaked figures where there were none? Coel didn't know but didn't dare confront them.

Another day he had seen the swirl of a grey cloak in the gloom of an alcove and heard a voice asking "Going somewhere, musician? How fast can you run? How far?" Coel had shivered, knowing he had lost this game and turned on his heel and continued his enquiries regarding the 'displeasing' merchant Renwick. Fleeing would be one mistake too far. The bard had a curious spirit, one which craved excitement and risk. It was a spirit Coel fought to suppress, but it was strong, cunning and refused to be silent. There was a wildness within which had on occasion landed him in trouble. Now it was enjoying itself.

August Renwick's trade was in flesh, for the man was a slaver. Coel felt a little easier, he had never met a slaver but he found the whole idea distasteful. Some criminals ended up in the slave pens but mostly the slaves were elves or humans stolen from their villages. Those with money could buy the flesh of another without. It had never occurred to him that the elves in his house were slaves. Uncomfortably he wondered how much his father had paid. What was the cost of freedom, what was the cost of a life? Servants were one thing, slaves another. Yet the task was not done and such men often hired guards, not only for their warehouses and waggon trains but in their houses, for thieves would consider such rich pickings worth the risk of a hangman's noose. Then, of course, there were the Witch-Hunters who would be more inclined to investigate untoward happenings in the dwelling of a rich man and patrols would be frequent. The Order encouraged the trade of flesh, particularly of elves, and, it was said, even took a cut of the gold. Fear was a powerful tool.

Sheltering in the shadow of a convenient doorway Coel watched the painted waggons, laden baskets and busy servants bustle towards a large townhouse despite the drizzle which coated man, elf and beast alike. The Master of Thieves had mentioned the household might be in need of an entertainer and judging by the amount of food and wine entering the house a feast of some sort was planned. Casually sauntering over, with an air of confidence he did not feel, Coel enquired of the elven dancers tumbling on the grass before a marquee of red and white striped fabric, and soon learned of the betrothal feast of the daughter of the household. Their human Keeper strode among them, ordering and commanding. They were his, to do with as he pleased, yet although his tongue lashed when one fell he spared the crop he had in his belt. A man to prize his merchandise he was not fool enough to mark his slaves before such an event.

Apparently, being a supplier of flesh paid well enough to provide a large house and spacious grounds even within the city. It had been a while since Coel had seen such promised luxury. Had it not been for his mistake he may have been the one enjoying such a feast. The goddess of luck smiled upon the bard, for once, when he made his way to the servants' door and asked, in his most charming manner, whether his lordship was in need of an entertainer.

A plump half-elven housekeeper stared at Coel, with a distracted, rather harassed look. She had thought to dismiss him, until she heard what profession he kept; looking over him, standing in the softly falling rain, the man seemed genuine enough. His cloak was not fine, but it was serviceable and looked reasonably new. He showed her the rebec and played a bar or two to show his worth. This man was good and suddenly the prayer she had muttered to the gods had been answered. Such a polite, charming creature could not be other than what he claimed, and it was true the minstrel hired to provide song had fallen to a gastric fever. She had been about to send out to find another when the gods had smiled. Her master would not have been pleased to find himself short a musician and he was not known to be forgiving.

***

Soft amber light danced from glowglobes, entwining with light wisps conjured by an elven woman adorned in flowing split silken robes as black as night; hair of plum-red tossed around her in a sea of curls. She was, apparently, part of the entertainment as she spun, juggling the wisps and their myriad lights and Coel suspected as much a slave as the elven dancers. The poor girl would be a Forbidden, her charms much sought after with her magic but not free, as mage and elf, doubly cursed. Her life belonged to someone else – certainly, it was not her own.

The elven dancers tumbled and weaved among the party-goers, whispering in ears and stroking cheeks, eager or desperate enough for coins to offer services not specifically hired. Their Keeper watched with care, but he knew his slaves would supplement their pay that night and drunken fumbles oft produced extra pickings. More than one guest would wake with pounding head to find beside him an elven form. Promises said in ale and wine, in the bedchamber and on the pillow were worth little to the receiver, but enough to cause consternation to the giver.

The wine had been flowing since before dark, these folks were far too refined to be drunk but they were distinctly merry. Coel had proven popular, he knew from experience, rich folk enjoyed tales of heroic deeds not their own, songs of love and honour and the poetry of times long past. The bride was young, barely sixteen with wide blue eyes and hair of gold, and her betrothed was a slight, rather bewildered boy of similar age. He was, it seemed, the only son of a fellow merchant and thus it served the House of Renwick and the House of Felden well enough to be united. What the two barely out of childhood thought was not open for discussion. Coel had watched as around the room they were paraded, like horses or slaves as the rich and mighty caroused. Now he saw things from the other side, outside looking inwards and he was not impressed. Servitude held many forms.

Coel's mind worked feverishly, where would such an item as he was here to find actually be? It sounded like a woman's trinket, a bottle for scent perhaps. At least, he hoped, it would be small enough to pocket. That was if he could find the bloody thing. Thieves often wore the clothes of a rich man as well as a poor man and with so many servants and the guests the room was crowded; his eyes searched around and he noted in among the guests finely dressed swords-for-hire trying and failing to look inconspicuous. They were trying to be subtle, as not to frighten or upset the guests but obvious enough to brook any misunderstanding. Even the large, scar-faced half-elf was donning his best attire. Failing to see another's weapon would not be a mistake Coel intended to make again.

So this place was guarded, and by ones who likely knew which end of a sword to poke in people. Coel considered it might be better to risk the blade of he who commanded the shadows than the likely beating he would get here if he was caught, so he would endeavour not to be.

Trellis tables decorated with cloth of gold wheeled in, topped with wedding gifts fit for a princess; fine mahogany chests filled with Far Isles silks, bands of gold set with gems and atop a fine rare white marble box stood a bottle of hollowed jade with a silver stopper. It was, indeed, exquisite and more importantly, it was seen by everyone assembled.

Coel swore inwardly, thinking the Thiefmaster might have known, after all, he seemed to know everything else. How was Coel to lift an item seen by all and easily recognised? The bard felt the world spin around him, as though this would be his last night; it was a feeling he had felt before when the shadows had risen and his legs carried him faster than he thought possible. He murmured a prayer to any obliging deity and called from within a sound he was not aware he even knew. Heart pounding Coel sang a song of glory, of deeds done and battles won, and hoped his voice did not waver. The music danced in the air, swirling like the mage and her balls of light, tumbling like the elven dancers and all onlookers turned as one to him. Magic was a fickle mistress and showed herself when it pleased her, for those in her embrace who called were oft not heeded, but this night Coel was her creature.

With distant eyes he saw a woman watching, transfixed and smiling; a dark beauty, plump and elegant. Her eyes like pools of clear blue water shone with tears. As the last notes ended, she held his gaze and he heard her soft exhalation and saw the tip of her tongue moisten ruby lips. Dragging his mind back from the chords of the song he recalled she was the mistress here, step-mother to the bride and wife to the slaver. She looked perhaps barely five or six years older than Coel himself and perhaps half her husband's age. Eventually with a smile like a hungry cat she nodded and continued to hold his gaze before looking away, confident he'd seen her.

Moving slowly around the room, conversing with guests she engineered to be close to the bard.

"That was quite a performance. You have a honeyed tongue, musician." Mistress Mariana Renwick's voice was soft, meant only for him and her blue eyes promised mischief.

Bowing Coel replied, "Thank you, Mistress Renwick, it serves me well on occasion."

A velvet gloved hand raised his chin and with a smile which crept across the edges of her mouth and sparkled in her eyes as she responded, "Is that so? Does it serve the ladies well also?"

Coel almost erupted with laughter at her forwardness, and his gaze flickered to the man of the house, whose attention was employed with the father of the boy soon to be his son-in-law. "It has been employed on such work on occasion, my lady, but perhaps your husband would find such employment a welcome change from his business," The laugh bubbled like a mountain stream, "He cares not for such past-times these days. His lady is a nurse, not a wife, yet he wears her like a trophy. She finds herself in need of other entertainment."

"Does she? Well, perhaps an entertainer is the man she needs," Coel replied with a wicked grin.

"Perhaps she would enjoy a private performance...in the parlour at the end of the second corridor; there is a statuette just outside and the key is in a hollow of the base." As the conversation rose around them her voice reached him at a whisper, as her lips brushed his ear, sending a shiver of desire straight to his groin. With barely a backwards glance she returned to her husband's side and just the soft scent of her lavender perfume remained.

***

Coel crept along dark passageways, ears pricked for the sound of guards or pattering of a servant's feet. Folks had returned to their own beds or, in a few cases, those of temporary companions; most of the elves had been sent back to their waggon and the tent which sat on the lawn, save those warming the beds of the rich and mighty. He wondered if the woman would be waiting for him or his night would be spent in finding a way to lift the item and be gone before the dawn. He sang about men who died a death of honour and glory and here he was sneaking through another's house looking to avail himself of the owner's wife and his goods.

Freezing with fear he heard a giggle suddenly become a soft sigh, soon joined by a deeper more masculine voice from a half-open door. Hoping they were too occupied to notice aught but themselves he moved on to the room at the end of a long corridor and almost fell over the statuette. Swiftly he groped about at the square base until his fingers found the cold iron of a key. The door swung open, with a disconcerting creak, into a room bathed in velvet darkness. Shapes were indistinct, hills and mounds of deeper blackness and occasional slivers of light from the moon shining in through a gap in the drapes. A flash of silver caught his attention in the silent room; then he saw the shape of it, beneath a cloth half tossed over.

"So, my pretty, there you are," Coel breathed. Before his courage deserted him the bard's fingers closed around the neck of the jade bottle, the object of so much difficulty, and he shoved it in the soft leather bag containing his rebec, then tugged the cloth over shrouding the gifts.

He had barely brought his nerves back under control and was just about to run for it when he heard the sound in the doorway. Tense he turned, expecting to be denounced; then he smelled the soft scent of his assignation.

"I was not sure you would be here..." she whispered, closing the door. He sensed rather than saw her as she moved closer.

"Nor was I, truth be told. Such a pretty thing, it took my fancy... and I could not resist." Coel was not sure if he spoke of the woman whose scent he breathed or the secret in the rebec bag.

A slender arm slid about his waist. "My husband is old, and he cares no longer for the pleasures of the bedroom... The wife of the slaver takes her freedom where she may. Now we were discussing your talented tongue were we not?"

"We were my lady... my gods you are a fine woman." Coel's hand swept upwards from her waist, caressing curves which were covered with nothing but a thin sheen of silk. He breathed her scent, thinking if this was his last night, he would make the most of the pleasure on offer. Coel's brain tried to tell him he should be running, but other lower parts of his person overruled it as a silk-clad thigh brushed against him.

Fingers teasing the tightness in his breeches Mariana led him to a shape close to the window; her free arm tugged aside the drape. "Take me in the moonlight, musician with the honeyed-tongue."

Silver light washed the frame of a chaise, and Coel murmured, "This was not part of the plan... but plan's change."

Mariana opened her mouth to ask what he meant to find it stopped by his own. Hungrily she devoured his kiss and moaned as his hand slipped beneath the silk. Coel breathed the edge of a song onto her jaw, the quiet hum of magic and music. Mariana gasped, never had she felt such an intense touch and she writhed beneath his hand.

Fingers teased a quim slick with passion and as Mariana moaned softly Coel nudged the rebec bag and its stolen contents beneath the chaise. Slowly his lips worked across one breast then the other, the chill air from the night peaking Mariana's nipples. Warm, moist mouth and cool breeze, a delicious combination as Coel's thumb flicked against her pip. The silken gown slithered down shoulders translucent in the moonlight and Coel's hardness pushed against the cloth of his breeches. Mariana reached for him, her nails against his flesh as she freed his straining manhood. Head tipped back Coel caught his breath as Mariana squeezed and began to stroke. One supple finger then another slid across her cleft, ticking the edge until she moaned, louder now.

A shadow flickered across the moonlight, and Coel stopped, "Hush woman, lest your husband hears."

"You think I care for him? You've started this fire do not quench it. He'll be snoring now and no trouble to us. If we have an audience, so much the better, think you not?" Mariana cupped Coel's balls, squeezing gently until he groaned, and his fingers continued their dance of passion. Soon enough the shadow was forgotten. Coel thought it was far too long since he'd truly tasted a woman of this fineness. Eyes closed he thought of *her,* the one whose name he dared not breathe. Mariana was of her kind, voluptuous and passionate. A woman who knew what pleased her and was not afraid to demand it.

"Now, mistress... what is your pleasure?" Coel murmured as laid her back on the chaise and slithered down, feathering kisses along thighs which did not often enough enjoy the touch of a man. As his mouth slowly crept upwards and his teeth nipped and teased Mariana cried, "Yes, oh gods, yes. Show me what else those lips may do."

Chuckling Coel murmured a song into her quim, lips gentle on her pip. Her taste was sweet; like the honey, she spoke of with such need. Mariana writhed, legs over Coel's shoulders as he pleasured her. Once he brought her to the edge of ecstasy then, pulled away and flipped her over. Slowly with one arm about her waist and the other hand tweaking her nipples, Coel thrust into Mariana from behind. Her silken gown slithering between them as their climax rose and he sang his song of passion for her alone.

***

Dawn tickled her amber fingers across Coel's face as the sun crept ever forward on its daily journey. He had crept away whilst darkness still provided a cloak and left the lady dozing and sated in the soft realm beyond pleasure. Utilising the lesser-used alleys, more than once he'd still had to dart into the comforting arms of a shadowy doorway. Coel was terrified, he had never stolen anything quite so obvious or from someone quite so important. Now the night was over and his passion spent reality had come calling. He was convinced the footsteps behind him were the Order bearing down to haul him away. Still, he could not suppress a grin, he had the item and he had spent the night pleasuring a fine woman. Once again, he thought if that night was to be his last night it would have been a worthwhile one. Never had the door of the Stuck Pig tavern seemed quite so welcoming. Coel crept up to his attic and stashed his booty beneath the mattress, for now, he was alive, and he'd done the job. He'd actually done it. Sliding beneath a meagre blanket Coel closed his eyes and thought of *her*, of them both.

In the throes of a dream was the hand he felt real or an illusion? Now only half asleep he heard a low laugh. Coel's hand found the dagger beneath his pillow — if he was going to be hauled away, he'd try and make it as difficult as possible. He was a dead man anyway so he may as well ensure he had company in the Other World.

"If I wanted you dead, lad, you would never have woken." A hand was held out to help him up.

Coel exhaled the breath he had not been aware he was holding. "It's you. Do you ever knock?"

The Thiefmaster laughed again, "Rarely. I believe you have something for me?"

The bard tugged the rebec bag from its hiding place, "It was not easy. Have they noticed?"

Sliding the jade bottle into his sleeve the Thiefmaster chuckled, "Aye, they have noticed. An item like that is very valuable. The slaver looks a fool, he cannot even protect the gift for his daughter's dowry and there were so many guests, who does he accuse? First the elves, then the guards, then the bridegroom's father, who apparently spent the night in the arms of an elven mage, much to the dissatisfaction of his wife. Oh, and someone apparently bedded the lady of the house, left her naked and quite aglow, all akimbo on a chaise. So now he is a cuckold too. It is just a shame it was not the virgin bride herself. That would really have made the night."

Moving to the door, he tossed a bag of coins onto the bed, "Services rendered. If the Witch-Hunters do decide to pay a visit here, then there is no proof of your theft. I am sure the lady of the house will vouch for you. I am impressed for I was not expecting you to complete the task. I thought you would run."

Coel grinned, "I thought about it."

Darius chuckled again, "Many do, few succeed. I will be using your talents again, bard."

***

In the comfort of his furnished rooms in the catacombs beneath the city the Thiefmaster relaxed and held up the small jade bottle before another cloaked figure, who said, "He survived it then? I owe you thirty gold pieces."

"That you do, my friend, aye that you do," replied the Master of Thieves sweeping up the coins.

His friend nodded, satisfied and poured them both a generous helping of brandy. "Now, what about the other matter? There is the question of the woman, she'd be very helpful to our cause."

Darius examined the fine golden liquid and contemplated his next move. "Aye she would, Shadowdancer, but you know I am needed elsewhere. There is that difficult situation with the Society of Hidden Secrets to be dealt with. We still don't know who among those who know has loose lips, and that's taking up most of my time. You need to return to Tremellic before much longer and most of my more experienced operatives are tied up or lying low. The Witch-Hunters have been a little too nosy of late."

The Shadowdancer shrugged, "It's your call. We can manage without Arabella of Jaeden – or hope for another opportunity. I'd take a night or so to deal with it but there is a slaver requiring my services on the way back – the last of those who were responsible for the Szendro attack and I have my instructions.

"Perhaps our little bard would like another outing, after all, he has a vested interest in seeing her safe.

Besides the fellow intrigues me. A human of his talents would be an asset."

Darius nodded, "Excellent idea. I'll give him the good news."

Draining his goblet, the Shadowdancer rose to leave, "Do you think he has the skill?"

"We will soon find out, if not I'll fetch the girl myself. I doubt she's going anywhere of her own volition for a while yet."

Part Three

Elsa, the female barkeep at the *Stuck Pig*, had been even more hospitable since Coel's outing. The bard had not only found a small bag containing new strings for his rebec, a flute of redwood and a plate stacked high with fresh rolls and goat's cheese, but all his shirts and breeches had been laundered and repaired free of charge. Coel had thought to take the payment from the Thiefmaster and find better lodgings until Elsa had whispered in his ear that it was 'most convenient' that Coel remained. She'd then spent an energetic night persuading him why. Both of them knew it was wise to remain in their current abode, the Thiefmaster was a busy man and did not wish for the extra work of tracking down his latest acquisition. Coel dared not ask Elsa how or why she knew him, but it became clear that she served the Master of Thieves and his shadows.

"I'll bring you some ale with your breakfast. We have just had a new batch – very special. Only for 'honoured' guests." Elsa grinned and waggled her ample behind as she tugged on the clothes discarded in the entertainment. "I've even put aside a special mug, just for you." With that, she left to go about her duties.

The missive had arrived via the pot of ale, the mug revealing a compartment in the handle. Coel had not initially noticed it until on becoming empty a small flange popped out and, curious, he worked the slither of metal until the thin paper slipped out. "Clever bastard, is everyone here in on this business," Coel muttered.

"Go to the Eastern Dock, beyond the rope yard. Wait for the dark sailor at the Sun's highest point. The shadows watch."

"What does that mean? Noon? That must be it. Why must he talk in riddles?" Coel shook his head, he was in deep and he knew it.

Flipping over the note he saw: *"Because he can…"*

It did not take a genius to work out who had sent the orders and Coel destroyed the scrap over the candle. "Smart bastard. Who does he think he is?"

Coel's inner voice replied, "The man who has your arse over a barrel, bard." Coel rose and checked the room, expecting to see the shadows move. He was, at least he appeared to be, alone.

Darkening his skin so that he looked more tanned, and less like the pale-skinned landlubber he was Coel then tugged his hair into a braid, of the type often worn by sailors. Selecting a plain shirt and breeches he shook his head, wondering what he was walking into. It was true no one had come to arrest him after the theft, and his life was now more comfortable, if not luxurious. "You're going to get yourself killed, Coel." He peered into the sliver of looking glass and replied to himself, "You forfeited your life once before, remember. That's how you ended up here. That mistake. That miscalculation which cost so much. Maybe if you help him out again, he'll help you."

Coel did not believe the bargain would be that simple. Men like the mysterious Thiefmaster did not play by the rules, at least not the rules Coel knew; he was not a man with a great many choices and Coel had to admit he had enjoyed the recent escapade, at least when the fear had subsided. He felt alive, needed even. The magic in him pounded, with every rhythm of his heart and in his head songs were born.

"You stupid bastard, you're going to go along with it, aren't you?" Coel muttered, wondering how long he'd been talking to himself.

***

The Eastern Dock was busy; Varlek was a thriving port and Coel strolled among the sailors, hauliers, women of pleasure and ne'er-do-wells. He tried to blend in, and the more he tried the harder it became. Recalling what had happened on that fateful night, which now seemed to belong to another time he halted, resting against a wall. The magic within him sparked and rose, as under his breath Coel mouthed the words of a song and the shadow of the eaves above him shifted. Another stanza formed and feeling more confident Coel looked around casually. Hardly anyone gave him a second glance, he was just a man going about his business. Coel sauntered over to a vendor selling hot food. With a start, the man looked up as Coel's fingers selected a pie.

"Gods man, where'd you pop out from? That's two copper bits, three if you want onions." Satisfied Coel paid the man and continued on his way.

As he rounded the end of an alley the bard almost collided with a Witch-Hunter patrol. So intent was he on checking he was not being followed, and sure he was Coel stumbled into the armed and armoured men.

"Hey, fellow, mind yourself! In a rush to get somewhere? Fleeing from something perhaps?" The Order man who spoke was young, perhaps Coel's own age but had the sharp look of one seeking something or perhaps someone.

"Check along that alley, Olaf. This young man is in a hurry. Perhaps he'd like to help us with our enquiries..." Coel's man motioned to another, who strode along the way the bard had just come.

Catching his breath Coel thought fast. "Apologies, sir. Not fleeing, I'm late for an assignation. My sailor, Johan Schmidt, returns to port today and he'll not be pleased if I'm not there. I've got something to tell him, something important and it was playing on my mind."

The Witch-Hunter looked Coel up and down. "What ship?" A man who was naturally suspicious, the Order soldier rested his hand on the hilt of his sword. This man did not look like the usual sailor's bit of tail.

"The *Gathering Storm,* she's fresh in from the Far Isles." Coel picked out the name of a ship he'd seen moored in the harbour and hoped they wouldn't check. "I'm to meet him in the Swordfish tavern." Coel knew it was a sailor's haunt – he'd played their once or twice and could find it again at need.

Olaf returned from scouting the alley, "Nothing, we've lost him."

"Hmm... convenient. Was someone following you? We seek a man in these streets. A dark-skinned elf with copper hair. He preys on bait such as you, sailor's flower.... He's wanted for living beyond the Enclave... and for theft and murder." The Witch-Hunter stared at Coel, who returned the look and hoped his face did not show the fear.

"I am not helpless. He'd not find me an easy take." Coel tried to look confident, and tough. Motioning the blade in his belt.

Letting his gaze rest on the bard long enough to make most men nervous the soldier said, "Let's see your papers, pretty boy."

Coel bit back his agitation, humming a song softly to calm himself, and as he felt around in his cloak for the required paperwork, he saw a figure step out from a sheltered doorway within earshot and nod its head once behind the Order men.

Thrusting the papers forward Coel wished he'd had the coin to get fake ones made. Sweat prickled his back and his throat was dry. Was he safe here, in this city of many souls and many sins? Had his crime followed him here. Which crime? The murder or the theft? Then he noticed the soldier held the papers upside down. Not every soldier could read, and hope dared to show her face.

"A dark-skinned half-elf, with copper hair? There's a trader at the edge of the merchant's quarter like that. He sells trinkets, cheap rings and pretty things. Goes by the name of Ran, or Raq maybe." Coel knew that there were many such meagre traders in the poorer sector of the merchants' quarter, and itinerant pedlars who scraped a living. Such an unusual man would no doubt be noticed, if he was there then he best find himself another haunt and if he wasn't then the Witch-Hunters would waste time asking questions in an area with little time for their kind. Coel had learned that love for the Order of Witch-Hunters was rarely forthcoming from the poor and desperate. "Raq," he knew was a derogatory word for Order, rat or scum in elvish. It was the only elven word he knew, and he took a chance the Order men did not even know that much.

"Eh, we docked at first tide! Where's you been, me handsome boy? Me cock needs your touch, it's sick of me own," the newcomer roared, throwing bear-like arms about Coel's chest. A bearded face grinned, and a wicked gleam sparkled in eyes of amber as the man who'd been lurking joined them.

Coel, trying to breathe through the man's embrace, replied huskily, "Johan? Johan! My old salt…"

'Johan' grabbed Coel's balls and the bard bit back the cry. "Don't we have somewhere private to be?" he managed.

"Er… yes. Your papers are in order. Raq you say?" The soldier handed back the papers and motioned them onwards. "Get on your way, citizens."

"Bloody hell, that was close. I assume it's not a mere coincidence you just happened to be here?" Coel extricated himself and looked at the retreating Witch-Hunters.

"Just out for a nice stroll. You looked like you were in a spot of bother with them soldiers. Good-looking chap like yourself, out alone in this part of the city? Either a bloody fool or a man with a particular goal in mind, I wonder which you are?" The bearded man asked, making sure Coel saw the cudgel at his belt.

"That depends on your perspective," Coel answered.

"And now… we are alone. Privacy at last. Tell me handsome, why I should not simply rob you and leave your pretty corpse in a ditch?"

"Because those Order men will probably be back before long. Because I'd take a guess your boss wouldn't be happy with that and because the shadows watch." Coel knew his luck would run out but he took a chance as his hand found the blade at his belt, just in case. He had no clue which of the thieves and cutthroats belonged to the Thiefmaster and which were self-employed or in the pay of another crime lord. He might be able to take this man, but he doubted it. Besides wolves hunted in packs.

Johan laughed, and a huge hand slapped Coel hard on the back. "Today is your day, pretty one. A word of warning…. Not all those who walk in shadow in this city are your friend. *He* has taken a liking to you, which is why you still live but be careful who you trust. Oh and if you fancy continuing our assigna.. assi… meeting I'll be in the Swordfish, sunshine."

Part Four

Life had become even more dangerous of late, Coel thought. More exciting, the inner voice said, the side of him which seemed determined to get the bard killed. *Shut up* Coel told himself, shaking his head as he continued on his way, a good deal more cautiously. Thieves, Witch-Hunters, randy sailors – if that was who Johan had been; what trouble had Coel ended up in? He wanted his old life which had been far more simple. And far more boring.

He was a pawn in a dangerous game in which he knew few of the rules and even less of the other players, and Coel tried to tell himself he didn't like it. Coel knew that was a lie. Once again, he thought about the woman he'd left behind, the cause of so much strife. He'd tried to forget her – after all he'd meant it as a simple affair like so many others – but she haunted him. What had happened haunted him. The husband's death had been an accident – hadn't it? Coel was no longer sure. Then there had been the elf. Sometimes he told himself it was just an elf, and better an elven neck in a noose than his own. Mostly he just felt guilt in the pit of his belly. Coel himself had not died that day but something within him had done so.

The sun was past its zenith when Coel finally arrived at the rope-yard by a circuitous route. At least once he thought he'd seen a shape behind him, but no one else had paid Coel any more than a passing glance. Muscled men with sun-bronzed bodies hauled rope, boxes, tools and items of machinery Coel could not guess the use of. He studied each worker – 'the dark sailor' wasn't much to go on. Besides he was late – he'd assumed the letter spoke of noon and it was past that – although Coel could not tell how far. Wandering around the perimeter Coel became nervous. Maybe he could pretend he hadn't received the note? Ah, no, he remembered the sailor 'Johan' — if indeed he was the Thiefmaster's man then that mysterious and deadly figure would soon know Coel had failed before he even started.

Becoming more despondent the further he went and the more lost he became, Coel turned along a narrow walkway to find himself in a small yard. Wooden sheds and sun-bleached cabins crowded in and the sounds of ale-drinking and song singing greeted the passer-by. Coel peered in through an open shutter into the roughest and merriest drinking house he'd ever seen. Painted crudely on the door was a bright red disk, rays of orange flowing across wood that had seen many days and most of those far better.

"Ale, barkeep," Coel said, having jostled his way in, taking the chance to examine every face he passed.

A swarthy, one-eyed man grinned a mostly toothless smile. "A copper piece for th'ale. There's meat pie or Maya's bread. Puts 'airs on a fella's chest does Maya's bread."

Barkeep Orson slapped the backside of the tall, comely and buxom trollish woman with spiralling horns, skin of jet and hair of bright amethyst spirals, who filled pint mugs and beakers and looked as though she could break up any fight single-handed. His eye ran over her, full of appreciation and adoration. "My missus, in case you were wondering, and she ain't on the menu."

Having no idea what Maya's bread might be but suspecting what the pies would be like, or indeed what might be in them Coel shouted about the din, "I'll have the... bread, please. I never trust pies." He handed over a couple of coins, trying again to search among the dockhands and sailors, and realising he had no clue for what or whom.

Faces of every shape and hue, elven, human and trolls laughed and quaffed and sang. Until arriving in the city Coel had never seen a troll, the mountain folk who tended to avoid the human lands – being no friends of the Order. He'd learned the Witch-Hunters usually left the trolls alone – their men were large, strong and renowned as warriors and their women clever, no-nonsense and feisty. Coel had even heard some of the menfolk could become wolves or bears at will, and another rumour stated trolls ate their enemies.

The trollish woman pushed a slab of grey-brown bread topped with a slab of butter half an inch thick towards Coel, who was trying not to stare at her. He'd never seen a female troll and had no idea they were quite so handsome. The ale she handed him, in a hand as large as his own was thick and dark as the tarred wood benches around the room. Bands of white stone and polished sea-pebbles adorned her horns, and the woman showed no fear of the rowdy men who surrounded her.

"Bloody hell, what's in this?" Coel spluttered as the syrupy liquid coated his throat.

"Maya's secret recipe…. Why do you think this place is so crowded?" the male barkeep told him, with a grin. "She's the gem of the mountains is my Maya. The best-looking woman and the finest cook this side of the Jagged Peaks."

Maya cuffed her husband, "You dopey old fool, I've never even seen the Jagged Peaks – I was born on Edgewise Street and you well know it."

"I'm looking for someone, or something called 'The Dark Boatman'. Know you of it?" Coel gingerly tried to tug the corner of the slab of bread. Then pulled harder as Maya chuckled.

"I might do. Who's asking, handsome? You don't look much like a sailor. Those soft hands and pale skin give you away, human," the barkeep warned him. "You want to watch yourself in these parts. There's deep water that will cover many sins and plenty of folks to commit 'em."

"Yes, I know, I've had one warning already today, a run in with the Order and almost got myself a new lover, a man with a beard you could lose a badger in. It's being an eventful day. I've a message to meet the Dark Boatman and I'm at a loss as to find him." Coel was becoming desperate. "Please. I have coin, I can pay..."

Maya took Coel's hand, palm up and let her fingers run across it, tingling and ticklish as the offered coins sparkled. He felt a crawling sensation, like ants running hither and thither, and found he could not withdraw his hand from her grasp. "A singer of songs, a teller of glories long gone and to come. This one comes from he who controls the shadows. Reluctant but brave. Seeking redemption for something and for someone. A hunter and hunted. Both one and the other."

"Coin, the magic word! Show our new friend to the balcony, my sweet. The view is good and the breeze from the Silver Sea brings out the best in the ale and the food. A musician? We need a good minstrel; the last chap.... Well, he plays with the fishes now, I told him Maya was a one-man girl, and he didn't listen." Orson grinned, toothless, but Coel was not encouraged by the humour.

The staircase to the upper floors was steep, certainly not to be negotiated when full of ale. Coel wondered how many had met their end at the foot of the stairs and finished up on the morning tide. From the outside, the building did not look high enough to accommodate any more than the common room and an attic, but they passed low-slung rafters, narrow doors and ladders which swung away at the touch of a certain plank or nail.

The wind whipped about Coel and his companion as she led him along a narrow platform, shielded from view but not from the weather by rough planking, thatch and sailcloth. "You are lucky, musician. You are easy to read. It's the magic in you, magic calls to magic. You've a song in your heart and a good soul. Many spend their lives denying what they are and hiding from the truth. He picks his agents carefully so you should be honoured."

"I didn't have a great deal of choice. I stole from him, and he has a way of explaining things..." Coel was relieved to actually tell someone.

Maya stopped, looking at the bard with new respect, "*You* stole something from *him*? That's priceless! Of course, he let you, but even so. You'll do well enough. I see a long, if entertaining, future for you.

"In there. Hopefully, the Dark Boatman hasn't decided to leave. Of course, I've been wrong before with the predictions.... Let's hope I'm not mistaken now." With that, she tugged some boards aside and motioned him forward.

It took a while for Coel's eyes to adjust to the gloom and he saw a shape hunched over something. "You are late." The voice was like velvet, but Coel could not tell whether it was male or female.

"I am," he conceded. "You are not easy to find. I wasn't sure you'd be here." Coel looked around the room, the furniture was old and worn - just a table, single chair and hammock. It was basic. A small, banded sailor's chest was partially covered by faded red sailcloth.

His eyes were drawn to the window and what stood before it: A long tapering wooden tube banded with what looked like copper but had a distinct glow around the bands. It loomed, there was no other word for it, on black metal legs, like a three-legged spider. Coel stared and got the distinct impression the object looked back at him. It was impossible but Coel had realised the impossible had become a regular occurrence of late.

A silvered glass hung from the ceiling but cast no reflection he could see. Deciding he was happy not knowing what the mirror, if that was what it was, did Coel found himself looking at the tube device again, in fact, he found it hard to stop.

"It's called a telescope. The elves used to make them long ago to look at the stars. Now I use her for watching ships. It's helpful to know who comes in. She watches and if I am away, I can view it on the mirror when I return."

"She? Her?" This was getting stranger and more unsettling by the minute. "I was told to meet the Dark Boatman here." Coel tried to see more of the stranger than just a shape. Then gave up. "I have no idea why." He was growing frustrated. One mistake he'd made that lifetime ago, and now here he was talking to a shadow in a room which shouldn't even be here and watched by a creepy elven artefact that was making his skin crawl. "I'd like to get my instructions and then get back to my nice safe attic, my music and what remains of my life."

The figure laughed, "Many of us wish for such luxury, few receive it. I am the Dark Boatman. I am your assignation."

Shaking a glowglobe up to a pale glimmer the figure stepped forward. A scarf hid most of his face, assuming it was a male. Coel still could not tell as a billowing shirt of black and red covered the figure's upper body, and strange baggy breeches left the thighs rather shapeless. Above the scarf eyes of golden brown watched, half a face of almost ebony black and the pointed ears of an elf peeked out of dark unkempt hair to the shoulders. The elf was a head shorter than Coel himself but broader and walked with the rolling gait of one more familiar with life at sea.

"Our mutual acquaintance is busy, dealing with an urgent matter, and bids me assist you with a little matter. There is an establishment – known locally as the Guildhouse – the haunt of merchants of the higher kind. It's well guarded and well patronised by men and women both. There is a woman there – who our friend wishes to be...extracted. She is the daughter of a wealthy man who has fallen on... difficult times. Her father wishes her liberated."

The Dark Boatman continued with a hollow voice, "It's very simple, bard. Fetch the girl and return her to the Sun. If you happen to learn anything of interest during your visit so much the better."

Coel expected there to be a catch but asked anyway, "Why can she not just leave?"

The Dark Boatman turned aside, "Her husband died, murdered, so they say. A man was hanged for it - an elf - but this woman, it was said she was in collusion. She was labelled whore and worse, hounded from her home and her baby son. I suppose you could say she is under house arrest; her father was so incensed, so angry he sold her to the 'Guildsmen'. She is bound by law. Such law cannot simply be undone with a change of heart. If she runs, she will be hunted."

"And what is our mutual friend's interest?" Coel shivered, in his head, he saw blood, lots of it and a knife in his own hand.

The Dark Boatman shrugged, "Who knows why he does what he does and why he chooses to save one and not another? He has his own plans and own instructions from even higher. We are but pieces in a deadly game and for it, we live to see the sunrise and the ships come in. Our kind gain some protection – we are the hunted, the haunted and the hounded. The shadows harbour many secrets – be grateful for it.

"The elf – the one who kept the date with the executioner was my lover. He was innocent – I know that as he was with me that day, but we are elves. I am wanted for smuggling. He was away from his master's house. What chance did we have? Did he have? Elves are guilty even when they are not. The woman was Arabella of Jaeden, daughter of Raoul Chandler."

Coel sunk down. "I'm sorry. Oh, gods I am sorry. Your man, he *was* innocent. I know who killed Osbert Cooper and it was not any elf." He could not bring himself to say it. Coel's passion – his arrogance had killed not one but two and ruined two more lives beyond those. Now he knew the Thiefmaster had not just selected him at random – he was beholden to him – a man whose business was the trade and manipulation of secrets.

The elf said nothing, and Coel dared not ask him if he knew the truth. "Where is this place?"

The silence hung between them, thick and dark, terrible as a storm waiting to break; an awful emptiness which would haunt Coel for a while to come. Now he understood why this man hid away, and he said quietly, "I'll do it. My life belongs to another now, should I lose what is merely borrowed then my song will end as an echo on the wind."

A velvet pouch landed at his feet and the elf stared at him, seeing his guilt and discomfort but feeling little pity.

"Expenses. If you rescind on the bargain you will die, have no doubt of that. The Thiefmaster's blade or mine – it makes no difference. If you try to run, you'll not get to the city gates. If you think to tell the Order, then a hangman's noose will be your next mistress. I've given you the name of the establishment – your first challenge is to locate it. You have three days and nights. Our meeting is over, now go and leave me to my ships and my grief."

Blood red clouds stained the sky, reflecting Coel's mood as returned to his attic at the Stuck Pig. It had taken him far longer to return from the dockland; Maya had waited some distance away staring out across the Silver Sea to escort him down. Every step had been a chore and once Coel had thought to step over the edge – redemption on the cobbles below, or in the churning waters. Only the thought of Arabella had stopped him, maybe this would be his atonement. Once again, he felt like a dead man walking, this time he didn't care.

"Who is he? The Dark Boatman?" he'd asked half considering if it could even have been the Thiefmaster himself in a clever disguise.

"A smuggler friend. That's all you need to know, musician. Make your preparations carefully and you'll succeed. Make just one mistake and the night will be your last." She had told him nothing else about his fate – refusing to elaborate further on her prophecy. But she'd been kind, providing some information and guidance, a bag of bread and a stoppered bottle of ale. As he'd left, she'd slipped a phial into his hand. "A little help if it's needed: two drops will cause sleep, four and the sleeper never wakes. Sometimes the song writes itself."

***

Careful enquiries had netted particular information regarding the Guildhouse – beyond the fine foyer and front quarters those without the required token or appointment would be turned out. This quality of merchants could afford competent guards and Coel discovered certain Witch-Hunters were known to frequent it, guests of the merchants. Officially it was a meeting place for the richer class of merchant, the traders in fine fabrics, jewels and even slaves. A respectable place of commerce and wealth – but Coel well knew appearances could deceive.

He wondered what the more strait-laced of the merchants thought of the Guildhouse's backroom activities – beyond the gaming tables and fine wines. He wondered what his own father would have made of it, a rather unimaginative man who understood his business but did not understand music, love or magic. And, he released now, a tyrant – intent on his own reputation and wealth beyond all else. Coel had wandered around the perimeter, having donned the new fine clothes the Dark Boatman's money had purchased. He knew enough of his father's business, and finally found a use for rather dull chit-chat he'd been forced to endure at gatherings and evenings of entertainment.

The guards were plenty, alert and well-armed. They did not look particularly amenable to desperate young men intent on stealing a 'bride' from the more secretive quarters beyond the main façade. Coel had considered trying a bribe but such a means of entry carried risk – even if he got inside it would be unlikely, he would be able to find the 'bridal suite' easily, if at all.

"You've got to get invited in – legitimately. It's risky but not as risky as trying to sneak past those damn guards," Coel told himself – noting the frequency of the patrols. "Now where do rich young men go to play whilst Father is feasting with his cronies?"

Coel was favoured with a good memory, and he recalled a tavern he'd found himself in on one of the first nights after his arrival. The haunt of the dissolute and the dandy.

***

"My father, he's a mean old bugger. He wants me to work for my allowance… where's the fun in that? Money is to be spent – let others do the earning," slurred the youngest son of the house of Halecombe as his goblet was again refilled from the bottle Coel had bought earlier in the evening.

"He's trying to marry me off to some horse-faced girl from Ignat's line. Not my taste at all…Besides – what do I know about young women?" the young man grumbled, grunting as once again the cards fell against him on the gaming table.

Coel smiled and leant to whisper in the young Halecombe's ear, murmuring enchanting words, softly breathing a song of love until the young man was firmly under his spell. "There are many ways a man may get the pleasures of a wife, or even a husband, without all the bother. Lessons given without judgement."

Halecombe shrugged, "I've been to the whorehouses, cheap trollops and fancy fairies the lot of them!"

Lips nibbling at young Halecombe's ear and one hand on his thigh Coel breathed, "What if I knew of somewhere else? Somewhere fine… not a whorehouse. It's a respectable house of entertainment where one can gain a 'bride' from among the elite. Somewhere your father would approve of…."

"Wosthisplace?" Halecombe mumbled. As Coel's soft words did their work. "Howjoogetin?"

"Sorry? It is noisy here... perhaps we should depart for somewhere we may...talk in private." Coel tossed a coin at the table elf and shoved the remainder of the brandy in his cloak.

They sauntered drunkenly arm in arm, beneath a sky just birthing stars. "I have lost my token for the Guildhouse, and my father refuses me another. There are women there so beautiful and men so glorious it's as though the gods of old walk among us. I'd take you but without a token, I'll be excluded.... Your father, on the other hand, is a respected man who loves his son. He'll grant you this." Coel breathed sweet nothings, into his companion's ear. "My love, we will have the best of times... and then after I'll show you something very special indeed...."

"Ask my father? Yes, I will ask my father. But he'll be cards that I've lost my money at cross," Halecombe mumbled, much the worse for drink.

Coel tipped out half of his remaining coin, "A present for my new friend. Your father will never know and if he gets you the Guildhouse Token tell him you'll marry the donkey. You can come and go as you please and I'll be your guest. We can get a private suite...Everyone is happy." Perhaps he'd even keep this sweet young pawn as insurance. Such a one as he would likely do Coel's bidding without a second thought. Coel smiled, he was enjoying this game.

Honeyed words and promises of pleasures to come, of games, and entertainment, of ample breasts and tight backsides woven on a song of magic ensured the young Halecombe was caught and played.

**

Crimson clouds roiled across the sky, the turmoil mirroring Coel's mood as he waited in shadow, a sword concealed beneath his cloak and the mysterious phial nestled in his belt. He'd heard a storm was due, and Coel could well believe it. Hopefully, it would provide some cover, and ensure fewer bodies were on the street.

He'd stashed a pack earlier that day - a spare set of clothes, a small cloak, a knife and rope. Young Halecombe had spent the morning sobering up in a room Coel had rented with what was left of his money and the afternoon closeted with his father. The bard tried to feel a little sorry for the pawn in his own game, after all, Coel himself was such a game piece, but his own emotions were in such tumult he simply went through the motions, saying what the love-struck youth wanted to hear. Music and magic could be cruel mistresses but love all the more so.

"I am Jacob Halecombe, this is my friend. We wish to enter," Halecombe told the guard at the gilded door, who looked far from impressed.

"So? Guildhouse is closed until sun-up." The guard was burly, brusque and bored.

"Does the name mean nothing? My father is a wealthy man; he'll not stand for your insolence!"

The guard looked over Halecombe slowly. He did not recognise this whelp. He looked rather dishevelled, rather young and rather naïve. "Not a great deal. The mighty of this city have sons aplenty, older and wiser than you, boy."

Coel rolled his eyes, the boy on his arm was sweet but rather foolish. The bard turned on the charm. "Apologies, good sir, 'tis my young friend's first time in such an establishment. He is rather nervous. We have the required...payment and my father, Witch-Hunter

Commander Terrence Samson, will be along tomorrow when he returns to the city. I understand you cater to the good men of the Order?" He held out the Guild Token. The threat of the wrath of the Order hanging between them. "I am sure we can come to an understanding…"

"You should have said, young master." The guard gave a salute and ushered them within.

"You never told me your father was a Witch-Hunter commander," Halecombe whispered.

"He's not, but would you take that risk? You have to know how to handle men of the guard's ilk." Coel grinned, "Guards tend to be of two or three sorts – bribery or flattery works, or threats. Of course, if you pick the wrong one it tends to get rather awkward."

Coel learned into his companion, murmuring into his ear. "Let me do the talking, my love. Do not contradict me and I promise you a night of bliss." His lips were soft and his words laden with magic and the enthralled young man nodded his acquiescence.

***

A high-ceilinged foyer, bedecked with expensive fabrics and paintings and displaying the crests of the various trades, the individual arms of particular families and the colours of the Order of Witch-Hunters greeted the two visitors. Coel scanned the crests, recognising a few among many and trying to commit as many as he could to memory. The Thiefmaster might be interested in the patronage of such fine families. There was no denying the show of wealth, power and allegiance.

"We have the required token, elf. We have recently arrived from the country and find ourselves in need of… entertainment. This is the best establishment in the city, is it not? Well known for the quality of the 'brides'." Coel slowly looked around, then whispered in his friend's ear as Halecombe squeezed his arm and mouthed 'when'. "Yes, yes... soon," Coel muttered, a little too loudly and mostly for the elf's benefit. Fortunately, excepting one elderly gentleman, the room was empty. Coel smiled and winked at the old man who returned the smile before the fellow made his way towards a side door and left.

"Ah, newcomers! Welcome to the honoured ranks of the Guildsmen," crooned the well-groomed elf. Many elves had an air of submission, however, this one could supply or withhold pleasures and he knew it. His was a far better lot than most elves, and many humans. He led them through curtained halls to a door, banded with iron, and locked firmly. Idly Coel wondered if such a lock would keep a certain master of thieves out. He doubted it.

The elf made a great display of producing a large ring of keys and unlocking the door and then, with a flourish, motioned them both through. "Apologies, young masters I did not catch your names and lineage. Such matters must be noted – for future reference you understand. The world is run by record keepers – I am First Record Keeper Alton – first among those who serve the Guildsmen. My family has kept the Ledger for a century and served the mighty of this city."

He stopped by a vast ledger on an oval table, quills and ink ready and waiting. "Once the records are sufficiently updated, we may proceed to the entertainment accommodation. We have many brides and grooms to please all tastes and our 'bridal suite' is matchless. Nowhere else can a young man find such quality."

"I do hope so. I have heard many tales of this place. I am Sebastion Samson, son of Commander Samson of the Order of Witch-Hunters and nephew of Eliza, wife of

Markus of Jaeden, merchant of that town. My young friend is Jacob, son of Augustus Cooper, quality barrel maker to the Lord of Reldfield," Coel replied, taking a gamble with the names. Markus was known to him and would likely be the sort to attend such a place as this, much to the displeasure of his long-suffering wife. Coel's own father had once been defrauded by the man, who wasn't nearly as honest as he appeared. "There's a particular lady with whom I wish to be acquainted – Arabella of Jaeden. I have heard she is the finest flower of that town, with a dangerous past. I like danger and a woman who knows what she wants. "

Halecome nudged Coel, "What about me?"

"My young friend would spend an evening amusing himself with a young bride and perhaps a young man, before returning to me. He is due to be married before the month is out and wishes to get some experience in the pleasures of women."

Coel watched as the elf completed the ledger, trying to peer at the selection of names. Surely so many names of the high and mighty would fetch quite a price in the right circles. *Gods I'm becoming like him,* Coel thought, and he grinned, despite himself. His inner adventurer was starting to enjoy this game.

The First Record Keeper bowed, "If you would care to wait in the library, gentlemen. Refreshment shall be brought whilst your friend decides on his companion or companions. We have the most exquisite portraits and accounts from which to choose. Any unoccupied companion may be seen in the flesh and at command they are yours."

Part Five

Arabella of Jaeden reclined upon a silken couch, fine gauze covering her ample curves, giving a tempting hint of breast and shapely thigh. Her garment obscured just enough to leave her a tantalising mystery but revealed more than enough to inflame the libido of those who came here. Dark eyes looked out from under a mask of painted gold and crimson and those eyes held sadness and resignation, lips painted crimson and skin dusted alabaster hinted at concealed beauty. About one wrist she wore a locket, the crystal inset holding in a soft lock of golden hair the length her finger.

The pelt of a great-cat covered a floor of marble squares and walls bedecked with rich velvet showed the wealth of the Guildsmen. She had little choice but to recline; a collar of thick black leather circled her neck, and a chain ran onto a ring set on the floor. A prison is still a prison be it stony cell or grand chamber.

Tears had long since been spent – first when her husband had been found dead, then more when she'd realised whose hand had held the blade. She'd wept when the elf had been dragged away protesting his innocence – but she'd not denied he had been guilty. She had not spoken in his defence. Not then. Her father had held his daughter close – believing her tears to be grief and shame at the loss of her man. He was correct but for a different reason and a different man. For the one she loved and lost was not the one whose name she bore. Arabella had not dared to speak out in the days after the discovery. Not then. Not until an elf hung from the gallows had she wept and wept until the truth was known. Just one mistake had she made – to love an unworthy man. Then another to hold her tongue to protect him. One mistake followed by another.

Part of Arabella had expected Coel to appear, to speak up. And when he hadn't that had been the greatest loss of all. That day her heart had broken, and little remained inside except the shame, sadness and the aching for her baby son. Her father had just told her, hollow-voiced, that she was to be removed to another property, 'to think on what she had done and the shame she had wrought upon them all.' Arabella had asked herself if he knew what she had endured in this place, then knew that he did. "Whore you were and whore you shall remain! I have no daughter of this house!" Those words had echoed over in her mind. Yet she had never realised his anger ran so deep.

Now she went about her 'duty' largely unfeeling. Passion could be real or unreal, and mostly it had become the latter. Once, she had loved and given herself completely, but now she moaned, and sighed and thought of her son and the pretended pleasure was enough to fool most, as she waited for the encounter to be over. But even now she found herself wanting the touch of another, to know she was alive and needed. Albeit fleetingly. Arabella pretended it was not the case but deep within she knew. Oh yes, her traitorous body yearned for the pleasure, for the desire but her heart was nothing now. Even the hatred had gone. This place was not as bad as it might be, Arabella told herself; she had earned the finest quarters in the Guildhouse. At first, she'd fought and tried to escape, refused to 'work' but somehow it had made her more desirable, both to the Guildhouse and its clientele. The 'bride who could not be tamed' as she become known.

As she viewed her fine rooms Arabella recalled the night she'd found herself in a dungeon of waterlogged stone, with nothing about her person but flea-infested rags, filth and worse.

"The choice you have, murderess, is thus – work for the Guildhouse as your father wished, and perhaps in time, you may earn your freedom and a life of relative ease. Or tomorrow meet the hangman. You are, are you not, a whore? You are a liar and who is to believe that you did not know what your lover planned? You're as guilty as he." The man who stood before her slowly scanned the stinking cell. "Of course, we could just leave you here to rot, or you could go to the lesser houses of pleasure – the Jaded Lady, the Unicorn or even just sent as the plaything of one of the Slaverlords. I can assure you, Mistress Arabella, you'd think this place a luxury compared to that option. You've heard of these places I trust?"

"How dare you! I am no whore! I am no murderess!" Arabella's voice wavered. But she knew, in part, he spoke the truth. She was an adulteress, and through her actions, her husband and an innocent elf had gone to their death. She had been a coward. Fighting back tears Arabella stood, knowing she was beaten, and too afraid to die. Her chamber at the Guildhouse had not been so bad; the food was good, she'd had fine clothes, and even books to keep her amused. It was, of course, still a cell but, Arabella realised she had little choice. Her mistakes had seen to that.

"Your life is no longer your own, woman. But don't give up what still remains of it." The Guildkeeper stood close, he looked her over. "You're a clever woman, an attractive woman. Some men would pay well for one like you, especially if you're feisty. Learn the trade and, just perhaps, you'll do well. Maybe you'd even get to see your son…."

Arabella gasped, her arms ached for the child and when she slept, she dreamed of his soft skin and little wrinkled face. "My boy?" Arabella's heart yearned for him, her breasts ached to feed him, for she'd refused a wet nurse and she knew then she'd agree. What use was she to him dead, or bringing further shame? Maybe, just maybe she could earn her freedom, and return to him.

"He's safe enough, so I hear. But he cries for his dam. A bargain then? Earn your keep and turn a profit with your body and you'll look on him again." The Guildkeeper was not cruel, at least compared to some. He did not waste lives, the lives belonging to the Guildhouse were his to manage and he was an efficient man. A bargain oft succeeded where threats would not

***

Young Halecombe had been escorted to one of the 'bridal' chambers, his excitement bubbling over, along with his chatter. He had chosen, from among the entertainment, a handsome elven man, with blond curls and a rather feminine face. "Meet me at sunrise at the edge of the merchant quarter, by the red well, sweet one," Coel whispered, weaving his spell.

Coel grinned, the young man was not a bad sort, and he was easy to manipulate. 'A pleasure-seeker from the idle rich' - that's what Coel's father called such youths when he was being particularly belligerent. Coel himself had been labelled thus, and then at least it had been true. The bard wondered where that young fop had gone, that time was long gone. An image rose of a bloody knife in his hand. Coel knew that foolish boy had died as much as the corpse he had made.

"The lady Arabella is the finest of our brides for those seeking adventure. Some say men are ensnared by her charms, and women envious. She'll please you, young sir, that's for certain." The elven escort, whom Alton had handed Coel to, was a fine, muscular specimen. And Coel noticed, armed. Coel along the bedecked corridor and up a vast curving staircase, he noted once again the colours and arms of several prominent houses.

Well-dressed men and women sat in booths at regular intervals - a sword, a whip and a cudgel each bore, though discretely. "Why the guards?" Coel enquired innocently.

"Some of our brides and consorts may require a little... Encouragement. And of late we have been plagued with thieves." The elf sneered, "You'd not believe it, sir, but even here it's true. The guards are merely a deterrent and protection."

Coel wondered how he'd get past. "Do they wait outside each door all night?"

"Some – it depends on the patron's instructions. There are chambers within also. A patron may even request their services or an audience." The elf motioned to a dark-haired male guard. "For example, Oscar is skilled at fellatio as well as fighting. His loyalty is unquestioned and so he commands a cohort. Marienne, in the second booth yonder, uses her whip to great satisfaction. Some patrons prefer that manner of entertainment thus the guards also may be hired as consort. Of course, they keep order here, also. Not all our brides and consorts are willing."

Biting his lip, so that the words which were trying to get out did not Coel nodded, hoping he looked impressed and intrigued, and feeling rather sick. He had bedded many partners, but none had been unwilling. Although, he considered, it may have been the case many felt themselves with little choice – like himself knowing a tumble might well earn coin, or a bed for the night, or even save a life. Choice, Coel had also learned hurriedly was relative.

Rare fabrics hung like the choicest gowns on a fine dame as they halted at a gleaming copper banded door. "Note the Far Isles silks of golden brown, and green. We have many patrons among the merchants of those regions, and one or two brides and consorts if one's tastes are for the exotic."

"This young patron requires the attentions of Arabella," said the elf to the burly female guard.

The chamber beyond the door held a bench, complete with rings for binding. The elf crouched and pulled a hidden lever, from the underside sprung out the second platform, angled thus legs may be spread. "Turn the lever, as wide as you wish. Or use the bench yourself, for your own pleasure!"

A dresser was opened to reveal a complicated many-layered set of shelves, which held every manner of tool and toy of pleasure and pain. "Yours for the use of. There is a captive healer about should you need it, simply ring the bell and ask. We simply ask you not to leave any lasting marks."

Coel peered into the semi-darkness and wondered about the use of some of the items, then wished he hadn't. "Er yes, thank you. I am sure to find something to meet my needs...."

***

Coel wished he'd thought of a better plan. Or, indeed, any plan at all. The door was guarded he was armed but hardly an experienced fighter and death seemed to be everywhere he looked. Listening at the door he heard the rustle of the guard's armour and muffled voices. But he was here now and committed, perhaps luck would favour him, or at least he'd take the guard with him when he died.

Mustering his courage Coel strode into the main chamber and stopped. He'd loved this woman – although he hadn't known it then. There she was, reclining on the furs. A prisoner and it was Coel's fault. Did he turn and run – a coward like had been before? Did he face his fear, his shame? With one hand on the sword in his belt, Coel tried to calm his heart and his head. A song rose inside – it had been their song – Coel had written it and sung it softly on a moonless night beneath her window, like the bards of old. Now he did not know what to say. His mouth flapped uselessly.

"That charm has left you then, along with your courage I see." Arabella arose, the chain rattled slightly, eyes cold they held Coel's gaze until he looked down.

She spoke the truth and he knew it. "I'm sorry. I know that probably means very little but truly I am. I panicked," Coel mumbled.

"Sorry? You destroy my life and you're sorry?" Arabella stared at him. "I loved you, Coel. I would have run away with you." She tried to reach him, angry, ashamed and the chain tugged tight. "I pay my penance for that mistake every day. I pay my penance when I see my son's face in my dreams and know I cannot hold him. My name is nothing and my life is nothing. I am but a whore to the wealthy and dead to my family. I thought more of you, Coel, but how wrong I was."

Coel slithered to his knees. "It's true. I'm a coward. I was afraid. I didn't realise…"

"Men never do. They just think with what's in their breeches or the scabbard they wear. Now, what are you doing here? Thought you'd come to revel in my shame?" The venom in her voice was clear enough.

"No! I'm here to get you out of this place. I didn't know or I'd not have allowed it. We could have run away – taken the baby..." He rose, a hollowness replacing the fear. Coel knew that his life was no longer his own, but he'd pay that debt one way or another. "Your father wants you back. I want you safe. If it makes you feel better the last few months have not been easy for me. I live at the edge of the law, I'm hunted. The company I keep is dangerous." It didn't sound convincing, Coel knew, as he spoke aloud.

The key turned in the door behind them, and the guard peered in, with a leer. "Everyt'ing as it should be? Do ya require assistance, sir...or perhaps an audience is what ya seek," she said, dark eyes scanning over Arabella. "Some of our first-time patrons like to be shown pleasures to be had. If t'is woman displeases feel free to punish her – you'll come all the better!"

Fighting back the bile Coel hummed softly until his heart calmed and his stomach stopped churning. "Food. I require food – the sensual sort; strawberries, good wine and Jaeden cheese." Voice soft and enchanting, Coel let the music with weave its spell, his smile broad and eyes glinting. Ever the charmer he drew his courage and recalled the phial the troll sorceress hand pressed into his hand. "Later you may join us...."

Arabella glared an even more baleful look and opened her mouth to say something then stopped. Despite what had gone between them, perhaps Coel was her chance of freedom. Besides, she recalled the beatings she had received at the guard's hand. Did Coel have a plan, as he promised, or was he simply weaving more lies? Arabella glanced around her gilded prison, and one hand felt the collar. Life in this place was a mere semblance of life, but it *was* life. Could there now be something beyond? But she remembered the cell, that terrible place. Then she saw her son, the image of the soft haired infant, and she smiled, tongue running over vermillion lips. Perhaps this *was* her chance.

Adorned with orange fragrant petals, and cloth of woven Shimmering Spider silk, the silver tray was laden with bright yellow cheese, fat strawberries, a jug of lemonade surrounded by ice – a rare luxury indeed - and gemmed goblets brimming with blood-red wine. Coel savoured the taste of the wine, with its citrus and exotic cinnamon. He grinned, beckoning the guard in.

"I find my pleasures enhanced with two women, especially two such gems." Coel winked at Arabella, unseen by the guard.

***

Sprawled across the luxuriant silken cushions, naked save a thick leather belt Natalia, the guard groaned, barely conscious. The welts over her back and behind fresh and red, over scars and bruises. Arabella raised her arm again, the crop in her fingers, sticky and trembling as the hand that held it shook with rage.

"Enough! I don't want another death at my door." Coel slid his hand around Arabella's and pulled her close.

"Get off me! You have no right to order me! You've no idea what I've suffered!" Her face creased in rage, pain and shame Arabella tried to pull away as Coel's free arm circled her.

Naked, he felt her warm skin once again and the passion he'd felt for this woman again reared but Coel knew even if Arabella would consent to lie with him again the guard would be missed. "Technically I do; you're mine, well Sebastian's, and thus I could order you. Or I could leave you here - bloody whip in your hand and a semi-conscious, drugged and beaten guard in your rooms...

"I can't imagine what your life has been, and I'm sorry for it – truly - but you're not a murderess! Look at her, look at her back! The drug will keep her out of it for long enough. We risk much already – maybe they won't look for you if you just run – but believe me when I say I know what it is to be hunted. Looking behind you, all the time. Never more than a night or two in the same bed. Never being able to tell your family you love them... or your woman." Coel held her as he dropped the crop and slid her silks over her body. Softly he sang a song of love, for her alone and unseen by the woman he held Coel wept.

Arabella squirmed but as Coel whispered in her ear his power eased her fury. Once she'd loved this man and still he could hold her spirit, though she fought it. "Get off me...." But the rage had left and, her face was a mask of sadness, Arabella looked around this room, as much a cell as the other. "My son. I want my son...."

Coel pulled himself back from the song, "Quickly – dress more appropriately. I'll deal with her."

The guard's hands were tied with rope from the play-box and Coel dragged her behind the couch, unseen at first entrance into the room. He pocketed the half-empty phial and rummaged for a suitable item to equip Arabella with a weapon.

"I have a sword, take one of these we may need it," he told her holding out a curved dagger and a cosh.

Dressed in the leggings, shirt and cloak Coel had stuffed in his pack, she picked up the crop. "This crop and that blade." The gleam in Arabella's eyes was dark, and deep, and deadly.

Coel hesitated and with, "er yes, alright," he stalked to the doorway.

The corridor was, at first glance, empty but Coel knew there were guards in the alcoves and so pulling the cowl of his cloak further over his face and telling Arabella to keep her head he motioned forward and locked the door behind them.

"Go where I go, do what I do and run when I tell you. If we get separated you must get to the docks. A tavern there called *The Sun* is a safe-house. Or the *Swordfish* and ask for Johan the sailor. Tell him Sunshine sent you. Don't wait for me," he whispered.

Arabella opened her mouth to comment and found his hand over her mouth. "Our lives may depend on it. Once we get outside don't mind what happens to me. I have...friends." Coel fervently hoped it was true as she nodded. Now he spoke it the plan seemed foolish, but he was in this game far further than he'd thought, and it was now play-it-through and hope he could bluff or concede and die.

Glowglobes cast their warm, and above all, bright light on the wide corridor. Coel hummed softly, just at the edge of hearing; trying to calm his turbulent soul, and his beating heart, which he swore sounded as loud as a drum. The music swirled around him, cloaking him and Coel's confidence grew. The guard loitering in the alcove beside one of the doors was dozing on his feet, much to Coel's surprise, and with a grunt he crumpled when Arabella's cosh firmly met the back of his head. Coel caught her hand as she lifted it again to strike him once more. "He's down, leave him. They might chase us if we run. They

WILL chase us if we leave a wake of corpses behind us. You're not a killer, I know it."

Arabella glared, but dropped her hand, and just motioned onward. Coel pushed the unconscious man into the shadow of the alcove and tearing a gag from his cloak he stuffed cloth in the fellow's mouth and tied it before tying his hands. "Now we move," he whispered, heading off.

Knowing there was likely a long and populated escape route if he chose the way he came he tried to call up what he'd seen as he'd been led to Arabella's suite. Coel cursed his memory and knew they walked a thin line. He recalled corridors and shadowed portices. "How well do you know this place?" Coel asked Arabella, suspecting he already knew the answer.

"I was a prisoner, remember. Do you think I'd have stayed there if I knew how to get out? There were Kepts or brides who were escorts to banquets and dances, I was not to be trusted so I was not among their number." Arabella shuddered as she recalled the awful stone cell.

"Yes, of course. I'm sorry. It's a fault of mine."

Coel felt the chill of the night air as he passed a green drape, just a touch on his face contrasting with the warmer air of the main building. The passage was dim, and they picked their way along. Coel bit back the cry of surprise and pain as his knee encountered a chest in the low light. They made do with the dimmed glowglobes casting a tenebrous light, which left them indistinct shapes.

"Do you actually have a plan?" Arabella asked, unsure and afraid. "We're going to get discovered. I've met the guards here – do not forget that. I care not for your good intentions, if they lay a hand on me, they'll lose their you-know. I thought you had a plan – I trusted you again. My mistake."

"Yes, of course, I have a plan," Coel soothed. Although he was not sure who he was trying to convince. *I just haven't finished thinking of it yet.* "How many floors here? Anything you have would be helpful."

"I'm not sure, at least three or four. I was not always in the quarters you've seen. The new Kepts and warmers are further down. Sometimes I'd have to teach one, or a virgin recruit would be sent to my room, for the customer to enjoy. Those with enough coin could have anything they wished. The Kepts would chat, gossip. In the early days I was a warmer." Her voice was low, sad and Coel looked away from her face not wishing to see the pain there. He could guess what a 'warmer' might be.

"Yes, that's helpful." Coel could think of no other reply. His mistake had left them both here, in this place of luxury, sin and shame. One a thief, murderer, and outlaw; the other a plaything, a slave, a whore.

"Window, bard, we have a rope. Find a window," he muttered, running his hand along the wall and feeling the drapes and tapestries even here. These were older, rougher and in places the wall was bare stone and cold to the touch.

Damn you, Thiefmaster. I'm not one of your shadows. But as soon as the thought surfaced another answered, *but you are, bard. You are.*

Shaking his head, and wondering, once again who or what this Thiefmaster was Coel's hand settled on a wooden frame. Deft fingers felt around, cold glass, wood and hinges. Only the rich and powerful had glass, most folk simply used wooden shutters of one variety or another. Many were badly made, but canny folk often lined the ledge inside with a selection of unpleasant surprises and would-be traps. Coel knew the barkeep at the Stuck Pig used a selection of old nails, shards of pottery and sticky resin. More than one patron had discovered this to their cost.

This window was not only a glass filled lattice, but the frames were carved, sturdy and above all locked tight. In the gloom the work to open them was almost impossible, so he took a chance and shook a glowglobe brighter. "Keep watch, but don't be seen. And find somewhere to secure the rope. We don't have much time."

There was a high chance even if he did manage to open the window the drop would kill them. *You're a fool, Coel. You're a dead man.* Coel began to hum, as he did when he was nervous. *Your life is forfeit. Hers is not.* "Sod it," Coel muttered, as the blade began to bend.

He glanced back, Arabella was fidgeting. For all her fierce words, he could see she was afraid, and that fear could get them both killed.

"Hey!" the yell froze them both.

The elf who had escorted Coel to his suite recalled this new customer – a Witch-Hunter's son, or so he said. The elf's eyes were good, even in the gloomy light. "And what *exactly* is afoot here? Off somewhere are we? Or perhaps you're just a thief!"

"Bollocks!" Coel cursed, and his free hand slipped onto the hilt of his weapon. "I was looking for my young friend, and we are just returning to the room..." As he said the words Coel knew they sounded foolish.

The elf sneered, "I think not. This is not anywhere near your room, and this is just an access-way. Guards!" As he yelled the elf reached sideways to pull at a cord unseen in the dimness.

Coel elbowed the window hard; the sound of breaking glass loud and terrible. Almost unbidden his other hand drew the sword. "Jump. I'll take care of this man," Coel said, knowing subterfuge had been lost.

"I'll stay and fight," Arabella replied, glaring at the elf who'd drawn a stout club.

"For once in your life, woman, do as I say. Jump out or get tossed out. Do it for your son, our son." Coel moved away from the shattered window, nearer to the elf and providing some cover for Arabella.

Arabella looked from Coel to the elven man closing on one another. It was likely the guards would come and she wasn't sure if Coel could handle himself with multiple targets. Yet she owed him nothing, and if he fell and she was caught her life was over, and her chance of freedom with it. Thinking of her son Arabella grabbed the rope and swung through the remains of the window, shards tingling around her and scoring the skin red on her arms. Blood flowed but in the heat of flight Arabella barely felt it.

Mud splashed around her and rain left cold drops on her face, but Arabella did not care. Never again had she thought to feel it and she stood as rain mingled with tears. Her ankle pained from a clumsy landing, and her face and arms scored with scratches from the glass. She was cold and would soon be very wet, but this was freedom! Arabella looked around, eyes trying to peer into the alleys and side streets then she ran, the elf's cry of "Stop her!" echoing in her head.

***

Coel appraised his options as Arabella disappeared through the now broken window: He could jump, hope he didn't break anything important and could snatch the rope and then run for it, or he could fight. If he took out this elf then Guildhouse guards would appear shortly and then the game was likely over. The elf dived forward, and the decision was made. Coel swung his sword, one eye trying to judge the distance to the window and the other watch his opponent. Whatever happened had to be swift.

"Thiefmaster – your girl is free. Debt paid. Now some help would be appreciated," Coel said quietly and not hopefully, wishing once again he was elsewhere. More through luck than great skill his weapon met the club wielded by the elf – leaving a scar in the wood. Being of a fairly wealthy background Coel had some training in arms but he doubted it would be enough against the likes of a man used to violence and disciplining the 'brides'. Coel groaned as the elf pulled a knife from his belt – the best of both worlds – blunt and edged. "You've no chance, pretty one. I've killed more men than you've had women in your bed. And as for your friend – the little flower – he'll not get out freely neither!"

With a grunt the elf kicked forward, foot impacting Coel's shin. He stumbled, clutching the drape for support and a cry almost escaped. Coel had and could fight dirty. It hadn't taken him long to discard the gentlemanly fighting he'd been taught in his father's house against the other wealthy boys – when a fellow was fighting to live any move was fair. There were no gentlemen in battle. At least not ones who lived to see another day. Coel began to hum, as he so often did when he was nervous. *This magic I've been told I have, where is it now? Magic, muse I need you!*

"He's just a lad. This is nothing to do with him." Coel's leg hurt but he sidestepped awkwardly as the elf swept the dagger towards him. *Shit, what am I going to do about him? This is not his battle,* Coel wondered, then dismissed the thought. He would be no good to Halecome if he was bleeding out on the floor.

The elf sneered, his elven hearing picked up the sound of feet heading in their direction. This boy would soon cease to be a problem. The elf dived, then spun as the club in his hand found Coel's kidney region. Pain blossomed across his torso; Coel slithered, one arm hitting the wall, his world a circle of hurt but his reflexes and his magic responded. Almost without Coel's bidding one foot kicked backwards and up, then jerked hard, taking the elf's leg out. As the man fell Coel's bruised elbow found its mark in his midriff and then jaw. The crack of bone against bone was awfully loud in the gloom.

Whimpering in pain, the fallen elf spat blood and teeth at Coel's foot. "You'll not get far...You'll be hunted." His voice was thick and low and breathless and as the man tried to rise, despite his injuries Coel shrugged. "Already am. But I have friends who'll look out for me," Coel hoped it was true but the little voice in his head reminded him Coel was merely just a sacrificial piece in a larger and more complicated game. "Shut up," he wheezed, trying to get a breath when breathing hurt.

His mind elsewhere Coel failed to see the elf strike with the knife – impaling his calf. "Argh! You bastard!" Blood scarlet and warm slicked slowly down his leg. Muscle ripped and flesh rent. Coel dropped, pain and desperation firing his anger. "You're no better than a slaver! Now, where's the lad? If he does not leave unharmed then the Thiefmaster will ensure this place falls in ash. I don't give a damn who your clients might be. I know well enough who runs this city." His hand snatched the club from the elf and tossed it aside; his good knee knelt hard on the elf's sword arm and he pulled it towards his chest, hearing the snap with satisfaction.

"The others are coming – you're finished..." yet the fight had gone from the guard and his voice faltered. "The Thiefmaster? You're his?"

Coel grinned nastily. "Perhaps you'll find out... perhaps not."

The bard knew he should kill this man if he was to be safe, but just could not bring himself to do so. The man was down, it would be some while until he was fit to menace anyone, or escort those with more money than morals about this palace of pleasure. Close to the man's ear, he breathed, "The shadows watch...silence buys lives."

As swiftly as he could manage Coel tore a strip of the curtain and tied up the elf who'd passed out from the pain of his broken arm being tugged and bound. Then yanked off the man's breeches and cape, discarding his own bloodied garments. His ears strained to hear the sound of others arriving and dragged the unconscious form into a darker spot; Coel's leg spiked with pain, and he wasn't sure he'd make the drop from the window, landing on one leg. Options were few and as he lurked, unsure, made use of the time bandaging his wounded leg. The limb bore weight, but only if Coel fought back the pain and the urge to vomit and moved slowly. His body hurt when he breathed, and he was not sure there was no internal damage from the club. He couldn't run and couldn't fight. That left charm, wit and luck. Coel had the former but doubted his store of the latter would last much longer. He needed to let Arabella get clear if she found herself in a tavern, or inn, perhaps a kindly soul would help. He shook away the other, darker thoughts chasing away his optimism. Varlek was not a forgiving city.

With care, he mopped up the worst of the blood, with the shirt torn from his captive and tossed it out of sight. In the gloom, he reached into his bag and fingers touched the small tub of face-paint. Coel grinned, his luck was holding. Face darkened and hair stuffed into a kerchief torn from his cloak Coel wished he'd had the looking glass. It would have to do.

Snatching away the glowglobe Coel tried to calm himself, calling up his music and letting the songs in his head quiet his pounding heart. The shadows rose up, enshrouding Coel, although so wrapped was the bard in his song he barely noticed.

"The bell came from this corridor – I'm sure, Wilf. Look – that window's busted!" The guard leant out – peering this way and that into the darkness. "That's quite a drop, even with this 'ere rope."

His companion looked thoughtfully at the rope. "Thieves again? Look – no glass on the inside. Wonder what they pinched this time?" He tried a couple of doors, one yielding a yell of 'do you mind!', a second nothing but silence. Coel held his breath as the man passed within a few feet of him but moved onwards. "Nowt here. Guess we better check outside… typical. It's pissing it down, again. Where's Iain, that snobby elf escort? I bet he's off with Esme again. From what I hear those two put rabbits to shame." The men chuckled as they headed away from Coel and back the way the elf had come.

Coel exhaled. His adventurous spirit had decided it had not done nearly enough to get Coel killed, so it had a plan. A bold, dangerous plan.

Part Six

Arabella was soaked to the skin, her cloak felt heavy and burdensome but she dared not shed it. There were those here who knew her, and the Guildsmen had powerful allies and determined servants. Even a wet cloak was some protection. She'd been lucky to get this far, and she knew it. Darkness pervaded, the alleys and backstreets unlit and building-crowded loomed in. She knew thieves, cutpurses and worse stalked these streets. Yet she was free and even the pain in her foot did not dispel the feeling. Arabella had not known how much liberty was worth until she'd lost it. Lost everything. Her hand rested firmly on the club beneath her cloak. These were not her streets, Jaeden was a smaller market town to the West, and even there some streets were unsafe after dark. She'd visited the city more than once, but seen from horseback, or carriage it looked very different. This was not her world.

Fear made Arabella desperate, but she knew this was the only chance she'd get to see her son. Breathing his name, she recalled the soft touch of his hair, the smell of his small body, and even his wailing was as music to her. Arabella would see her son or die trying. Luck had brought her to the crossing of ways and taking shelter in a doorway Arabella wrapped her ankle and tended to the worst of her cuts. The docks? Where were the docks, she asked herself? She felt in the pack Coel had given her – fingers closing on a smooth round item, a slightly warm sphere and the cold metal of a rattling tin. More than once she thought she'd seen someone stalking her. Then as she'd turned and peered into the darkness the shape had vanished. In her terror was her mind playing tricks?

The glowglobe was rather old and dim but it was a light source, and Arabella had never been so grateful. A candle would not stay lit in this weather, a lantern would be better but needed oil and could not be stuffed handily in a strap or belt. The tin contained coins, no means a fortune but enough for a cheap bed, or a hot meal in a tavern. The other item was an apple. Arabella grinned, apples had been their favourite food. Particularly when Coel had clumsily scaled one of her husband's apple trees to find a particularly juicy specimen. He'd almost fallen out, scuffing his arms in the struggle to get down. She'd kissed his raw skin better and then made love to him beneath the tree, daringly in sight of the gardens. That had been another life. Another Arabella. She bit the apple hard, the fruit taking the brunt of her ire.

She thought back to her time here, the stories her father had said of the city and the tid-bits from her customers. The docks were to the east and north of the city – she knew that but where was here which way was North? The way directly ahead was a street of shops, booths and small-holders. A chandler, the linen-seller, the ironmonger; at this time the units were dark but likely guarded. She turned aside – the alley was narrow, refuse strewn and she saw the sign of a tavern.

The *Potter's Wheel* was the sort of drinking establishment frequented by craftsmen and workers of the lesser sort. The ale was passable and the food edible, but it was not, by any stretch of the imagination, a place Arabella's social type would usually visit. Rough and ready, with rotting rushes on the floor, spittoons and urine buckets against the walls and a smell which mad the nose turn up, if not shut down entirely. It was, however, dry and would likely provide her with information. How far she had fallen for the mistake made in the heat of passion! Just one initial mistake had damned her to another, then another and the web of folly encircled her, tightly. Here and now she was a whore on the run and choices were few and so she took those she had. One hand on the cosh beneath her sodden cloak Arabella mustered her courage.

Trying to look around, without appearing to do so Arabella saw a man in the colours of the Order of Witch-Hunters, his tabard emblazoned with their emblem. Legs stretched out towards the fire and a dripping cloak tossed over a nearby chair he relaxed with a tankard and a plate of pies and bread. The man was young, perhaps barely beyond his cadetship, but around him was a circle of emptiness. Even the junior Order members were feared, if only because they tended to travel in pairs or groups. Where one Order man walked, another stepped beside, before, or after him. It would look suspicious if she turned and left so Arabella walked to the bar. She was, after all, just a woman caught by the weather and after a drink. That was all. So, she fervently hoped.

"Cider, if you have it," she said, attempting to keep one eye on the Order man.

"No cider, but the ale's good, miss. Not a good night yonder, is it?" The barkeep grinned toothlessly. "Maybe some food to fill yer belly? A pie with actual meat, or cheese?"

"Ale will suffice. I am looking for the docks – I have to... have to meet my husband there. It's so dark and wet, I lost my bearings." Arabella had become a reasonable liar, but she felt eyes watching her. She was the only female, save a girl of perhaps nine or ten collecting pots and delivering drinks to the tables.

"The docks are dangerous at night for a woman alone, miss." The barkeep glanced over at the Order man, "You require an escort?"

No... I would not want to disturb anyone. I just need to wait out the rain and then I'll manage, but I don't know which way to go." Arabella shook her head, rather too hard. "

The barkeep thought Arabella was too eager to dismiss his offer. He looked at her, face shadowed by the hood of her cloak, mud-splattered and limping. "Four copper pieces for the ale, and for a shilling, I'll throw in a pie and the information. Can't have one of my patrons ending up face down in the water, now can I. The missus would have my balls."

Arabella avoided his gaze, this wasn't going as planned. Not that she'd actually had a plan. Finding herself wondering about Coel, and needing him, she shrugged off the thought. "Your wife? Maybe she'd have some dry clothes? I have money." She rattled the tin, then carefully took out a silver shilling.

"Possibly – though she's bigger than you." He bellowed a name, and a tall, well-built woman strode in from the back. "Ella – this woman wants to buy some clothing... she says she has none."

Seeing the barkeep's gaze on her Arabella simply squeaked, "Mine are wet through and torn. I don't wish to meet my husband like this."

Ella scrutinised the woman standing before her. "I've got an old cloak, and a clean skirt you can buy. Your husband? He has not sent someone to collect you?"

Arabella wished she'd just continued running, but as the pain of her sprained ankle reminded her of why she had not, she tried to remember the lies already told. "His ship is due in today, and I thought I'd surprise him. We're not long married you see. He just a deckhand, he wouldn't have the coin for it, even if he knew I was coming, which he doesn't."

"The docks are north and east, but there are thieves and worse about – I am sure yonder Order man would see you safe. Which ship is your man on?" The woman's gaze pierced Arabella's soul, slowly unravelling the lies.

More and more nervous, Arabella tried to eye the Witch-Hunter who was now looking at the events unwinding at the bar. "Ship? Oh yes, it's the…the…*Sunshine.*

"I'd rather just meet my man in person. There's a tavern…he mentioned – the *Swordfish* or something. He'd just go there, I am sure." Arabella knew she was beginning to sound desperate but if she ran, then she'd be chased, and probably caught

Ella smiled, and her eyes glittered. "What a nice surprise for him. It will be a shilling then for the refreshments and two more for the clothes. Perhaps you could get a message to him to meet you here?" She flicked a glance at the Order man, "Joseph, yonder, likes his ale and his pies and what he DON'T like is trouble. His mate will be along shortly no doubt, girl. They hunt in packs…"

The barkeep shrugged, this tavern was not a sailor's haunt and *Sunshine* was as good a name as any for a ship. Grunting from the firm prod in his back, Jonas decided it was not his business if this woman was up to no good, so long as she wasn't caught doing it on his premises. If she could pay then that was enough. What he didn't know couldn't be used against him. Besides – he was far more frightened of the wrath of his wife than the inebriated Witch-Hunter waiting out the rain.

Taking her money he motioned to Ella, "You can go out the back, no funny business though. If I find anything gone I'll call the Order."

Opening her mouth to protest she was not a thief Arabella's brain, already in self-protection mode replied, "Thank you, barkeep. I can wait out the rain, I need no escort."

The man grunted, thinking this woman strange and suspicious, but feeling his wife's eyes on the back of his neck the barkeep waved her though. "Always a soft touch for those in need, Ella. One day you'll be the death of us!" he said, voice low. If he'd simply thrown this woman out, or called the Order he'd never hear the end of it. Ella was a good woman, and fifteen years of marriage had taught him who ruled in their relationship, but he sometimes wondered if there was more to her kindness and if it truly would bring them both down.

She merely smiled and took Arabella's arm. "Don't mind 'im - Ella'll get you sorted."

Part Seven

The creeping pain of Coel's wounds slowed his step but his music, his daring and his magic moved him on. The bard knew he was simply the creature of something he barely understood, something forbidden, and yet the thrill of it roared through every sinew. Songs rose and fell within him, music tumbled from his lips. The magic, for such it was, craved freedom in a world which hated it, and so the now dark-skinned, limping man walked daringly through the halls and corridors.

Through an open doorway stood a woman, naked and gasping as her customer took his pleasure, but it was at Coel she looked. Coel found himself staring back, and he bowed, before striding in to plant a kiss on her rose-tinted lips and weaving his song about her. Enraptured by his song and demeanour she tipped back her head, trembling as the climax took her, and her eyes never left him. Her partner snapped his head up to see the interloper and was also ensnared in the song. One hand reached for Coel, beckoning, and the bard saw the longing in the man's eyes, even as his pleasure reached its peak in the woman whose quim he pounded.

The part of Coel which was sensible, cautious, and self-preserving yelled inwardly, *what are you doing! This is not the time for lust. Damn you, Coel, get you gone.* He simply smiled and his mouth said, "Another time... for now, cause me a distraction. I need to leave here in a hurry."

The woman slithered from beneath her partner, "Three doors beyond my rooms, there is a servants' passage. It's hard to see, beyond the sabre-cat pelt. It will take you to the level below. Then there is a window with a loose catch." Bare as the day she was born the woman, dark skin glistening told him. "I've got out that way."

Suddenly the woman darted from him, and out of the door, still bare of skin, and ran along the corridor. The man grunted, tired from his exertions, but his feet began to pound the floor after her. "Hey! I'm not finished with you! Damn woman!"

"Catch them! Catch her. A man his age should not run after girls, it'll finish him!" So rose the voices edged with amusement and concern.

Coel slipped onwards, wrapped in shadow, embraced in music. Physically he was exhausted, in pain and fear, but the magic within him pushed ever forwards. The servants' passage was not, in fact, difficult to find. So, shrouded in his magic and music was Coel he failed to notice the young woman with arms filled with laundry. Almost colliding the girl stumbled and the linen tumbled around their feet. Macee opened her mouth to scream, as the wild-eyed, limping man whose words poured around him in a jumble of sound, pushed by in the narrow passage. Before she knew it her mouth had closed and she'd stepped aside as the man kicked away a dirty garment and strode on. Macee knew she should report him; all the servants had been under close scrutiny since the recent thefts but somehow Macee found herself stepping back and allowing him to pass. She simply bent down and scooped up her washing.

The window was small, but as the Kept had told him the catch was indeed loose. Merely a minute went by before Coel had the window open. The night was dark, wet and he could not tell how far the drop might be. With a curse, Coel tugged off his cloak; the knot was clumsy, and he was not convinced it would hold, but he could hear shouting as the magic began to wear off. Whether it was his decoy or for Coel himself the bard had no idea but decided he did not have time to find out. Muttering a prayer to any god who might be listening he swung into the darkness.

***

Arabella had been dressed in a skirt of faded green, with yellow trim which had seen better days, a thick woollen man's shirt and provided with a short wool cape. It was not rich, but it was dry, warm and respectable enough. The clothes were too large, but with some creative pinning, tucking and tying she looked larger than she was and far less elegant. It would pass as a reasonable disguise.

"You're a striking girl, easily recognised." Ella scrutinised her. "Cut your hair, and there's some powder for your face in the drawer."

Wanting to refuse Arabella hesitated. "Have you done this before? Helped woman like me?"

Ella's eyes darkened, "Aye, once or twice. Fellas too. It's not just girls who end up in those places, or worse."

Reluctantly taking the shears Arabella replied proudly but unconvincingly, "I do not know what you mean."

Arms crossed, her protectress said, "Really? Which was it? The Street of Red Lanterns is some way from here, but there are other...establishments and private houses of pleasure. Your perfume and the look in your eyes - I've seen it before and smelt it before. My sister was taken, years ago now. Ended up as some man's plaything, he and his friends, until she was no longer wanted. He got bored, tossed her into the street with nothing, save the clothes on her back. And then she ended up in some brothel or other. She'd been taken on the road to Jaeden – slavers, you see, plying their filthy flesh-trade. We got her back, eventually – eight years – eight. The woman who came back to us was just a shell. There was nothing she could say to the Order, not with her... skills. She was a Forbidden, I think it's called. My father and brothers had not stopped looking, not for one day. And poor old father died of shame and hatred of the slavers. Sarina had that look. The look you've got. Like a locked door, or a cloak of shame. It's not just elves that get took."

"I'm sorry. What happened to her?" Arabella could not help but ask and was afraid that her past life would be obvious.

"She lives in Redwall – the southern city –with a woman who fishes on the river and makes nets. They have an elven orphan child to raise. He must be oh... ten or more now. But she never speaks of it. She sleeps badly and she's very wary. Or so her lady-friend says. She has a life and a decent enough one, but not the life she should have had. Not the life that was stolen."

"The Guildhouse. They have...entertainment for those with enough coin, and enough influence." Arabella looked wistfully at the pile of hair at her feet. "Thank you for helping me. And the others." Arabella had known there were other people like her, other girls and young men who serviced the rich and mighty but for her part, Arabella wondered if she'd deserved her punishment. Her mistake had been to love another than her husband, and then to keep silent because of that love, and her own self-preservation. Because of Arabella and Coel two innocent men had died. The anger that she'd felt – the hard-done-byness – began to abate. "Isn't it dangerous? Helping me, with that Witch-Hunter a few feet away?"

Ella shrugged, "Probably. But what he don't know won't hurt 'im, as they say. And Witch-Hunters don't know a lot in my experience. Now let's get you gone before people start asking awkward questions. Besides I'll keep him busy, that one comes here quite a bit, Ella knows how to deal with a lad missing his mother."

Pressing some money into the woman's hand Arabella told her as Ella shook her head, "I've not much left, but I have my pride."

***

The peep of day was just edging its way across the sky when Arabella found the *Swordfish* tavern. Being lost in the docklands was risky even in daylight but to her surprise and relief, she had not been disturbed, although she held felt as though she were watched and followed. This was the case, had she known it.

Even at this hour, late or early depending on point of view, there was raucous laughter emanating from the establishment. *The Swordfish* never closed if there was money to be made from ships and their crew. And just occasionally clandestine cargo needed a safe place to rest before it continued its journey.

"Sunshine sent me, I am looking for Johan," Arabella said loudly, trying to make herself heard above the din. The room heaved with bodies, most somewhat pickled by this time. As with many of the dockland taverns, people of shapes and colours of all sorts jostled, sang, fought and caroused. Some looked for work, some recounted fantastic tales of faraway lands, and others simply stared morosely into their ale. As she'd entered a few faces looked up, but women of one sort or another were common here and so the sailors went back to their pursuits.

"Sunshine? Don't know any 'Sunshine?' One-Eyed Pete, Bull Sisci and Whaleskinner are still 'ere but I am not sure there's a 'Sunshine,'" the serving woman, waved a tanned and scarred hand about. "Ships come and go. The Order is pressing men these days. Silver Sea is getting dangerous – pirates, mysterious storms, and monsters if the tales are true."

"No, no! I need to FIND a man called Johan. Sunshine sent me. Johan will know who I am. I've come a long way to meet him, I'm soaked and tired. I think someone is after me." In her desperation tears shone brightly, even in the tallow-lit space.

Taking pity on Arabella's disappointed and frightened expression the woman continued, "Sit down, lass. I'll ask. We have several 'Johans'. It's a popular name in the North."

A large hand placed a pewter flagon of ale next to Arabella and a large, bearded man followed. "Well, you're Sunshine's bit of skirt, are you?" Johan looked the woman over. "He owes me...something. He'll know what it is. I remember me debts, and what I'm owed. I'm Johan of the *Gathering Storm*."

***

Slithering in the mud as he landed Coel cursed again. He could definitely hear shouting from above and the nearby streets, and it was getting louder. The alley was almost completely dark and he dared not risk a light. Pain sang its song in his body and the adrenaline and mysterious music had departed and left Coel with barely enough energy to move. Now he was just a desperate man, hunted and on the run in the dark. Coel was exhausted, every muscle groaned, and every joint was afire. Had he known it magic demanded a price, and the bill was now due. Feeling his way forwards Coel found the end of the alley, but not before more than one encounter with the wall, unidentified objects that seemed to be made entirely of sharp corners, and sticky, stinking mud.

At least one collision had sent a crippling pain over his back and around his chest and ribs and midriff already pummelled took extra damage; Coel had pulled himself up more through sheer bloody-mindedness than anything else. Keeping to the narrow lanes and the gaps between the buildings his route was slow but ever further from the Guildhouse. *I hope she's safe. After this, after everything, I hope she's safe.*

Every step became more difficult, more painful. The world wobbled like he'd had far too much ale and Coel wondered when he'd started to fall."I must see the Sun, tell him she is free. The sun... where is it? I've lost the sun." Words thick and confused Coel's breath was shallow, his voice weak and sounding far away. He was a spectator watching this mud-caked, shambling and stinking creature wind its way unsteadily onwards. And Coel could see its odds were not good.

His foot caught an object in the darkness and Coel stumbled, kicking over something wet, and stinking of the privy. The wound in his leg began to bleed once more, and as he staggered on the damaged limb finally called the cards. Unceremoniously Coel continued to slide until he was face down in the reeking mud. He wanted to sleep, more than anything. Except perhaps a bath. Then darkness came.

Part Eight

Sunlight slithered slowly through the gap in the roof above Coel, and the warmth of it caused him to wake. Trying to pull himself through the fog of unconsciousness he groaned, throat dry like parchment. Someone he couldn't yet see tipped a waterskin to his lips and the bard drank greedily, of the sweet liquid.

"Steady, not too much at first." The voice was soft and comforting, and oddly familiar. He wondered what the pungent smell was, wafting about the room. Coel realised it was him. Or at least the salve covering his re-bound leg and the warm, tingling feeling in his ribs.

Coel lay back, feeling the woollen blanket on his skin and the surprisingly soft cover beneath him. Part of him was amazed he still lived. "Where am I? How did I get here? I remember the darkness, and the pain but everything else is a bit foggy."

"You're safe. Orson found you in the gutter and carried you back. You'll live." Maya grinned and ran her hand over his bandaged, but otherwise naked chest, the mage slowly trailed her fingers. As Coel knew she was magical and was not in a position to report her skills she risked its use. He'd been in a real state when Orson had deposited the stinking, feverish and half-dead form in the backroom of their establishment. Magic exacted a price, and it had been known that price was high indeed. "Likely you'll carry the scar on your leg for some time, and I'd not try anything too strenuous for a while if I were you. You need rest and someone to fuss over you. Your clothes were burnt, can't have a stench like that frightening off our customers, but the rest of your things are in yonder trunk. There are food and more drink for you, the tonic will fortify. But if the Order comes a-looking and asks questions you're Orson's nephew Richard from the country."

"I feel terrible. Like someone hollowed me out. I can breathe better now, thank you. I am in your debt. I'll help in the tavern, I'll run errands and I'll entertain to pay what I owe." Coel managed a smile and Maya bowed her head to him.

"We can talk about that another day. For now, your keep is paid." She took his hand, her fingers trailing their magic along the lines. "The visions were...undecided. So occasionally it doesn't hurt to give fate a nudge in the right direction. *He* likes you. He must do, not everyone gets such protection." Maya had no need of saying the name. They both knew of whom she spoke.

"The woman, Arabella? Is she safe?" he asked after sifting his befogged memory of recent events,

"Aye, she's well enough. Your friend Johan saw to it she was returned to somewhere more...suitable. He says you owe him an assignation. Oh, and I understand there was a lad, Halecombe was it?" Maya winked at him. "You're busy, that's for sure."

"Damn. I hope he's alright. Sweet soul, but very foolish." Coel felt guilty, now he was here, and the excitement was over he knew he'd used the young man for his own purposes.

"Don't you worry, he's safe as well. You wrote to him and told him you'd been called away. You'd contact him in a week or so to renew your friendship and support him before his marriage." Maya was trying very hard not to laugh at the look of total confusion which crossed Coel's face.

"I did? Oh yes, is there anything *he* doesn't know?" Coel asked, wearily. The truth descending on him slowly.

"He doesn't know everything, no one does. But he does make sure he knows what's going on with all his units," the troll woman replied.

"We are all just his toys, aren't we?" Coel said, knowing the answer already.

Maya laughed. "For sure. But we are alive because of it. Folks like us need friends such as him, and his allies. We are 'beyond the law' of this land and so we must make our own. Sometimes a little…recognition is needed of this. You have talent, and the magic has chosen you. Don't waste either and you'll do well enough. Now rest."

***

The waggon which had taken Arabella of Jaeden to her father's holding had not been luxurious, but to Arabella, it might well have been a golden coach pulled by the finest horses. The journey had been slow, for the trader had been about his own business as well as that of the Thiefmaster. She'd passed this route before, but now she noticed the beauty of it. Freedom was a gift she'd not part with again. As the track wound away behind them Arabella realised that she'd not been truly alive before – simply going about her business, then trying to survive. Now, she decided, every day would be a worthy day, a worthwhile day and she'd thank the gods for it. They'd been stopped once on the road and asked for papers but the trader, whose name she'd soon learned was Kristos, had handed over two signed and sealed sets and been waved on his way. Arabella decided not to ask too closely. If the worst happened and she was caught then she could not reveal information she didn't know. Some things, she'd decided were simply best accepted as what they were.

She'd stopped at a small local temple in one of the trading posts and tossed the remainder of her money into the collection urn. Arabella was not pious; religion in Erana was for most something nodded to, invoked at need and then dismissed when the crisis was over. The Witch-Hunters tolerated it – for not even, they dared openly defied the gods but it was not encouraged. Someone had to help feed the poor and desperate, and deal with the sick and so many temples harboured priests and priestesses and other such workers in the service of whichever deity was prominent, or in many places the gods in general. Even Witch-Hunters needed healing and succour from time to time. As with many things in a land of forbidden magic and hidden rituals the Order turned a blind eye if it served a purpose on that particular day.

The walk along the lane to the cottage took her a lifetime, as the past, and its shame flowed from her and something new took its place – hope. She saw a child, blond hair flapping in the breeze as he happily played with a small cat in front of the house. "Elijah!" The words tumbled from her as the child looked up, squinting at this stranger. Running she scooped him into her arms, breathing in his smell and then she too looked up to see a man watching them both.

"Welcome home, my girl. I was a bloody fool. I made a mistake when I was angry. Do you forgive me, daughter? My Arabella!" Raoul Chandler asked arms open. Tears glittered as he beheld the young woman who'd brought such unhappiness to his household, such shame. But he knew most of that shame was his.

Arabella stepped back, looked around and replied, her voice cracking, "Yes, we all make mistakes. Just one is enough."

About the Author

Author Bio:

British-born Alexandra Butcher (A. L. Butcher) is an avid reader and creator of worlds, a poet, and a dreamer, a lover of science, natural history, history, and monkeys. Her prose has been described as 'dark and gritty' and her poetry as evocative. She writes with a sure and sometimes erotic sensibility of things that might have been, never were, but could be.

Alexandra is the author of the **Light Beyond the Storm Chronicles**, *and lyrical fantasy series, and several short stories in the fantasy and fantasy romance genres. With a background in politics, classical studies, ancient history and mythology, her affinities bring an eclectic and unique flavour in her work, mixing reality and dream in alchemical proportions that bring her characters and worlds to life.*

Social Media links
Amazon Author page http://amzn.to/2hK33OM
Facebook Author Page http://bit.ly/FB2j0bbdZ
X (Twitter) http://bit.ly/Twi2hJZ3h9
Goodreads http://bit.ly/GR2iqokvK
Library of Erana Blog http://bit.ly/Blog2iAWL3o
Linked In https://www.linkedin.com/in/alex-butcher-8342ab13b/
Tumblr https://libraryoferana.tumblr.com

If you enjoyed this, please check out A. L. Butcher's other works.

Set in the world of Erana

The Light Beyond the Storm Chronicles series – an adult fantasy/fantasy romance series, with a touch of erotica.

The Light Beyond the Storm Chronicles – Book I
The Shining Citadel – The Light Beyond the Storm Chronicles – Book II–
The Stolen Tower – the Light Beyond the Storm Chronicles – Book III

Erana fiction

Tales of Erana: Myths and Legends

Tales of Erana: The Warrior's Curse

Other short stories:

Outside the Walls – a short historical fantasy fiction
Co-authored with Diana L. Wicker
Expanded edition.

The Kitchen Imps and Other Dark Tales – six short tales of mayhem and mischief
Echoes of a Song (Legacy of the Mask Tales)
Tears and Crimson Velvet (Legacy of the Mask Tales)
The Watcher
Dark Tales and Twisted Verses
The Last Forest

Anthology pieces in the following:

Heroika: Dragon Eaters

Heroika: Skirmishers

Lovers in Hell
Mystics in Hell

Stand Together – Poetry and Prose for Ukraine

A Splendid Salmagundi, which won the Indie Book Bargains Award for Anthologies in 2012

Wyrd Worlds

Wyrd Worlds II

Nightly Bites – Vol II

Shattered Mirror – A Poetry Collection
Beyond the Shattered Mirror

.

Printed in Great Britain
by Amazon